RIP

In the Beginning

D1520537

Written By

ROBERT HARRELL

PAGE PUBLISHING
Conneaut Lake, PA

First originally published by Page Publishing 2022

Any similar names, places or events in this book are purely coincidence and for entrainment purposes only.

ISBN 978-1-6624-8512-1 (pbk)
ISBN 978-1-6624-8513-8 (digital)

Printed in the United States of America

CHAPTER 1

It's was a beautiful fall Sunday as I'm driving through the countryside to town to see my children before I go to work. Hoping Crystal's boyfriend isn't there puffing his chest and being a douche, thinking he's warding me off from jumping Crystal's bones. I divorced her for a reason.

As I round the corner of my once home street into this peaceful neighborhood, I see a handful of people out mowing their lawns and bagging leaves of their well-manicured homes. I pull into the driveway to see my oldest daughter pulling weeds and cleaning out the flower beds. Emily looks up and sees me pulling in, and her little face lights up.

Emily, fifteen years old going on thirty, drops everything and runs to me as I open the door, her yelling "Daddy!" and leaping into my arms. She holds me tight, trembling with excitement as if I had been gone for months as I had in the past when I was away on deployments. Her precious little face looks up at me with tears of excitement in her beautiful eyes.

"How is my girl?" I ask her.

"I'm so glad to see you, Daddy, I've missed you!"

"Honey, I just saw you last week." I chuckle to myself. "Is everything okay? How's school?"

"Yes," she says. "I just wish you were still living here. I miss getting up in the middle of the night and having our talks over a bowl of cereal. You know, our us times." Her sad little face looks down at the ground.

"Well, I have you and Cindy next weekend, and we can stay up all night and talk and play games," I say. "You still dating Trigger?"

She giggles and says, "Dad his name is Travis, not Trigger!"

"Trigger, Travis, petado, potatoes."

She thrust her hip at mine, playfully bumping me.

I look up to see Crystal standing on the porch watching and smiling. Looking just as beautiful, perhaps even more so, as the day I married her. I take Emily's head in my hands and firmly kiss her forehead and look into her bright green eyes and reassure her, "You have my number. You can call me anytime for any reason."

"I can't wait until next weekend," she said. "Is Rose going to be there?"

"She may pop in, but she has to work. Next weekend is you, me, and Cindy time. Okay?"

She reaches up, grabs my head, kisses my forehead, and looks at me then her mother. She whispers, "I hope you marry Rose, Dad."

Tears well up in my eyes. I know how much the girls love Rose. I smile and hug her one more time and walk up to the porch to Crystal. She greets me with a hug and a half smile.

She says, "Cindy is in her room, having tea and crumpets with Eeyore."

We walk into the house, and I said, "I guess I'll go crash her party."

I walk down the hall, looking over my shoulder, and ask if she was doing okay and if the micro d——ck is being good to her and my girls.

She says, "Don't start, Rip!"

I just laugh and open the door.

Cindy looks up from the little table with a huge overstuffed Eeyore that I won her at the county fair. She squeals out "Daddy!" and jumps up and dives headfirst into me as I kneel to her. Hugging and kissing. My heart melts.

Cindy, being a typical six-year-old, starts jabbering a million miles an hour about everything at once in one continuous sentence without stopping to breathe. Then she stops and looks into my eyes and says, "I have my clothes packed, Daddy. Can we go now?"

I look into her innocent little face, knowing she was confused about what weekend she was coming with me. I said, "Honey, that's next week, not this weekend."

Her little bottom lip pouts out, and tears well up in those big green eyes. My heart breaks as I hold her close to comfort her as she gently sobs. I hold her head into my neck, reassuring her. "Next weekend, it's just you and your sister and me."

She pulls back and looks straight into my eyes with half a smile and says, "And Rose too, right, Daddy?"

"No. I'm sorry, baby. Rose has to work, but I'm sure she'll pop in to see you. You know she loves that little face of yours."

Her little face lights up, and she says, "Good. I love her little face too. She's so pretty and sweet and so cool." She turns and picks up a tiny cup of imaginary tea and carefully hands it to me. "Here, Daddy, have some tea with me and Eeyore."

I carefully take the cup from her little hand and hold it by the tiny handle. I start to put it to my lips, but she abruptly stops me, saying, "Dad, it's tea, not coffee!"

I smile and extend my pinky and watch her smile.

After I finish my tea, I tell her to hug me. "I've got to get to work."

My littlest princess walks me out, holding my hand. Emily comes over to say goodbye. I pick up Cindy in my arms and squeeze her tight, as I wrap my free arm around Emily and hold her close, kissing them both.

"I will see you two ladies this week, and we'll plan out our weekend, okay?" I say. "I love you both so, so much. Forever in a day."

They echo me. I get into my Jeep and drive away. As I look into my mirrors, I can see them both hugging Crystal, and I feel a twinge of pain in my heart as I round the corner. I don't normally work on Saturdays, but I have a new client who had been out of town all week and was anxious for my expertise in setting up a security perimeter, so it was going to be a short day. This leaves me time to go down to the bar and have a couple of drinks with my best friend and fellow teammate, Boomer.

As I walk into the bar, I see Boomer was quick drawing beer against some poor unsuspecting drunk on a bet. Boomer had his sixth beer down before his competition could finish his third.

Boomer isn't a big man, but he is wiry and fast as greased lightning, and we always have each other's backs. We serve on the Teams together on multiple missions. He specializes in explosives ordinance disposal and deployment. He can make your toothbrush explode with no effort or sweat.

Apparently, six beers were the end of the bet. Boomer let out a belch that was grotesque while onlookers cheer him on and make fun of the poor sucker trying to refrain from puking.

I anxiously look around for my favorite female human. Scanning through the crowd, I finally see her. Rose, my sweet Rose. Coal-black hair and bright beautiful blue eyes and a body that God himself formed to perfection with his own fingers. Her beauty illuminates from her heart and soul and shone from her perfect smile. She is my friend for life and everything any man could ever possibly need or want in a woman.

She sees me looking at her, and she smiles and makes her way to me, wrapping her arms around me and hugging me tight enough to squeeze out any pain or sorrow I have. Can't help but feel like melted butter.

Suddenly, we hear a crash and bang behind us. We turn around to see Boomer taking down the poor sucker who lost to him shooting beers. The guy's friends are making their way to the fight to help their friend.

Shaking my head, I yell at Boomer, asking him if he needed some help. "I've got you, brother, if you need me."

As two guys try to take him down, Boomer throat-punches one while kicking the other's knee, effectively breaking it. Oh, did I mention that Boomer is also a master at hand-to-hand combat? We have been sparring partners for years.

Rose looks at the three groaning men lying on the floor and shakes her head, saying, "Damn, I wish I could fight like that." She looks at Boomer and says, "Thank you for not breaking anything this time." She laughs and walks away.

I turn my head as she walks away, thinking, *I hate to see you leave, but I love watching you walk away.*

We grab the troublemakers and drag them out of the bar and into the parking lot and told them in no uncertain terms to not return tonight. Hail a cab and send them on their way. We go back in and find a couple of stools at the bar and watch Rose work, and we talk. Occasionally, Rose will come over and chat with us.

She asks, "Have you seen the girls?"

"Yes," I say. "I stopped over this morning before I went to work."

"When are you getting them?"

I reply, "Next weekend, and by the way, they both are just crazy about you. They asked if you were going to come next weekend too. But I told them you were working, but you may pop in and see them."

"Aw," she says. "They are so precious."

"They certainly have my heart," I say.

We have a couple of drinks, and I have to head home as I haven't been sleeping well. I wrap my arms around Rose and kiss her face and head home, leaving Boomer behind.

CHAPTER 2

I am abruptly awakened by a pounding on my door. Snapping awake, immediately grabbing my .45, and carefully heading for the door.

Peering through the peephole, I see Boomer looking around like he was being hunted. I open the door, and he quickly comes in and shuts the door. Boomer is very rattled, and he doesn't rattle easily, let alone be noticeably upset.

"I'm so glad you're home, Rip!" he says. "I don't know how to say this, Rip. Something terrible has happened, and I don't know how to tell you."

"What?" I ask, looking at his face fighting back the tears. "What, Boomer? What happened?"

He looks into my eyes and breaks out, "It's Crystal and the kids, Rip. They're dead! They're dead!"

Everything freezes in time. I feel my heart break immediately into a million pieces. My eyes get blurry, and I grab him by the arms. "What are you saying?" I frantically blurt out. "This is a piss-poor joke, Boomer! Tell me it's a joke! You're not serious, right?"

"I'm sorry, Rip, I'm so sorry," Boomer says. "I wish I was wrong. There was a fire. Your house burnt down, and they found the bodies inside. They found two adults and two children. I watched the coroner carry them out." He looks down, and tears begin running down his cheeks.

"There has to be a mistake," I say, trying to think. "There has to be a mistake! My babies!"

6

Boomer looks up at me and says, "Rip, my sources say that the fourth body was you."

"Well, it's not," I say. "It must be Rick!"

Shaking his head, Boomer says, "No, Rip. They're claiming it looks like a triple murder and a suicide. They're saying that they think you killed them and then yourself."

"That's crazy," I say. "I'd never kill my babies. I may not be happy with Crystal, but I still love her. I'd never!"

Boomer looks at me and asks softly, "You didn't go over there at all after you left the bar, did you?"

"No, I came straight home and got a shower and went to bed! Why are you asking me this? You think I did this?"

"No, Rip, but I had to ask. I trust you fully. Listen to me, Rip. We need to get you out of here right now and hide you until we find out what the f——ck happened. Something smells here. I'll put the word out on the street and see what our people are hearing. Let's move. Go grab only necessities, grab any necessary weaponry, and grab toiletries. When the detectives get here, it needs to look like nothing is disturbed or missing."

I grab my long rifles and M60 and hand them to Boomer. I grab what ammo I could carry, leaving a couple of handguns behind. We put them in his Tahoe and decide we need to leave my jeep somewhere relatively close to my old neighborhood to support their suspicion, thus buying us time to gather information.

My mind is racing and my soul is hurting beyond anything I've ever felt before. Trying to concentrate on our goal, I drive to a 7-Eleven about two blocks from the house and park around the back where there are no cameras. Then I get into Boomer's vehicle and slide down out of sight. I tell him to drive by the house.

Boomer says, "Okay, but I'll go down a cross street, not down your street. Don't want to be spotted."

We drive down the cross street, and I look over to where the house once stood. The remains are lit up by the floodlights on the emergency vehicles. I cover my face and sob as we drive off.

Boomer and I sit, trying to figure out what happened and why. We keep going back to "It had to do something with Rick." He has to be responsible. If that wasn't him in the fire, who was it?

Later that day, Boomer gets a phone call from a friend. As he's talking to him, he looks at me and shakes his head no, saying, "So it wasn't Rick then? Okay, well, keep your ear open, and let me know ASAP if you hear anything at all. Thank you."

He hangs up the phone and looks at me. "It isn't Rick, and he has an alibi. Maybe we are looking at this all wrong, Rip. Maybe *you* were the target. We've pissed off a lot of people that would love to see our demise, and if they can't get you, then your family would be their best shot."

"Boom, I'm wondering how the police were so sure that the other body was me," I say. "They couldn't have gotten any DNA results back that fast."

"I don't know, Rip. My understanding there wasn't much left of the remains to even get a dental ID."

The thoughts of my poor babies flood back and overwhelm me, and I fight back the tears. This time, I feel rage beginning to stir deep inside, and I know someone was going to pay dearly for this.

Days go by until we get any more news, but at least it gives us a direction to start. Police still say that it was me who did this. We get a call that informed us that the word on the street is that it was a hit job from the WarDogs.

The WarDogs is a well-known violent gang heavily involved with human trafficking and heroin sale on the streets. When I come off the Teams, I do some intel gathering for the CPD on the WarDogs trying to get that sh——t out of our schools. It is starting to add up if somehow they have found out that it was me who infiltrated their little boys' club. There would have to be a leak in the department. There are only four officers who know anything about this operation.

Boomer hands me a piece of paper with a number on it, saying, "This is Dr. Hess's number. Dr. Hess is a great and trusted plastic surgeon. It's time for you to disappear from the planet as if you did die in that fire. I'll work on getting you a new ID. By the way, the funerals are tomorrow. Are we going to go?"

Of course I can't not go, but it will have to be from a distance as not to be seen. I call the doctor and get set up for surgery the following week. Then I will have to go into heavy training and tuning up my skills. After all, it is time to go into battle.

I look at Boomer and tell him, "Get me a team put together, buddy."

The following day, I go to the cemetery and stay on the outer edges and watch, wearing dark sunglasses and a hoodie. Boomer goes to the funeral and stands beside Rose, with his arm around her comforting her as she cries.

All four coffins line up, side by side, one draped with an American flag. The onlookers surrounding the caskets as the preacher spoke. Many familiar faces sobbing and comforting each other. I can't hear what is being said, but nevertheless, it is a beautiful service, ending with the taps being played and a twenty-one-gun salute.

As everyone leaves, some put flowers on the girls' coffins and Crystal's but none on mine. Rose and Boomer stand there for a couple of minutes after everyone else goes back to their cars. Then they go to each casket and stand for a moment, and she places a white rose on each of the girls' then places a pink one on Crystal's, then she stands at mine. Bends down and places a black rose on the coffin, then turns and returns to her car.

My heart is broken as I silently say my goodbyes to my loves and my life.

The following week, I wake up out of surgery, my face and my hands wrapped up in bandages, and I look like a mummy. There is a lot of pain, inside and out, but I push through it and am anxious to get the bandages off and see the results. Dr. Hess reconstructed my face and said that my own mother wouldn't recognize me. He also changed my fingerprints and altered my vocal cords to change my voice.

Recovery is slow and painful, then the day comes to remove the bandages. The doctor sits in front of me, slowly unwrapping my head. He gets the bandages off and removes some gauze stuck to me and cleans my face up, inspecting his work.

He hands me a mirror for the moment of truth. Smiling, he says, "Well, it's certainly an improvement over that mug you had."

Boomer watches over his shoulder with a look of amazement. He looks at the doctor and says, "Great job, Doc! Definitely an improvement." He chuckles.

I look into the mirror and feel like someone else is looking back at me. There are some bruising and discoloration, tenderness, and puffiness, but overall, it looks great.

After a couple more weeks, pictures are taken for my new ID. The name was Robert Ivan Polin. Yes, my abbreviation is still Rip.

I chuckle and look at Boomer and say, "Now Rip stands for Robert Is Pissed. Boomer, get everyone together for a meeting. We need to plan out our strategy. We need weapons, communications, vehicles, and, most of all, money. Being as the WarDogs started this fight, then they may as well pay for it out of their pockets. When we hit their heroin kitchens and pimps and anyplace else they have a couple of dollars, what are they going to do, call the cops?"

Boomer and I begin a regimen of intense training and toning to condition ourselves for what is coming. Sparing and enhancing my hand-to-hand combat skills. Hitting the range and burning up plenty of ammo. Boomer and I learning from each other's abilities. My specialties were guerrilla and urban warfare.

The day comes for me to meet the team Boomer had put together. Each has their specialties and expertise. True American patriots, all but one serving in the military in multiple combat campaigns. He put together a team of twenty rough and tough men and one woman. They line up for introduction, and most meet each other for the first time. These guys come from all over the country to be here, and I am humbled. They are sick and tired of being sick and tired of the punks and thugs who were taking over our streets, and they want to make a difference.

Going down the line, I meet these guys one at a time as they introduce themselves to me and state their services, ranks, and abilities. Until we get to one giant whom Boomer addressed as Bull.

The Bull stood approximately six feet eight and an easy three hundred pounds. Coal-black hair and black eyes with a stare that would scare the hell out of anyone as he looks down at me, making me feel like a midget.

Boomer begins filling me in on Bull.

I interrupt him. "Doesn't he speak for himself?"

Both of us look up at the Bull.

Boomer smiles and replies, "He can speak, but he rarely does. When he does speak, you better listen."

As we continue down the line, I'm observing one guy outwardly and obnoxiously checking out our one female member. Stepping back and scoping out her perfect little form and undressing her with his eyes and acting like some street hood and making stupid faces.

We get to him. He steps back into the line, being cool and not caring how immature he looks. Smugly, he introduces himself as Cowboy and states his long list of abilities and talents.

Then he asks, "Is this a team, or is this some sort of a Girl Scout troop?" Looks over at the baby-faced blonde standing beside him with a bright smile on her face.

She looks over at him, smiling from ear to ear with a twinkle in her bright blue eyes.

Boomer steps back and tug at me to do the same. I step back as Cowboy reaches up to touch her chin, saying, "We need to go dancing and have a couple of drinks." Makes suggestive comments.

Calmly, she plays along. "You like little Girl Scouts, huh, big boy? Maybe later we can go practice making little brownies?"

Cowboy says, "Yeah, baby, you know what I like." He goes to put his arm around her, smiling the whole time.

At the speed of light, she throat-punches Cowboy, effectively collapsing his windpipe and dropping him to his knees. She holds him up by his hair as he's struggling to breathe, looking back at her smiling little face. She says, "Don't you ever touch me or disrespect me or any woman ever again, or I'll leave you to die just like this."

His face begins to change color, and he is approaching unconsciousness. She grabs his throat right where she had punched him and manipulates her fingers, and he begins breathing again. Choking and gasping, he regathers his senses. Embarrassed, he stands back up and stands his position and looks into her eyes and apologizes.

Boomer looks at her and says, "This is Aubrey Lee. Ms. Lee has multiple black belt degrees in multiple martial arts, including Krav Maga."

"Impressive," I say. "Krav Maga is an extremely difficult art to master. How well did you assimilate this skill with the rest of your talents?"

Boomer speaks up. "According to the Israeli consulate, Aubrey was one of the best students the Israeli military had ever trained. In effect, Ms. Lee is our official personal ninja. She can breach any secure facility undetected. She doesn't use firearms, only tools of the trades."

"Very impressive, Ms. Lee," I say.

Looking across the team, I welcome them all and say, "You people get acquainted and get to be friends. Learn from each other, and build friendships and trust. Your life may very well depend on the guy or gal standing beside you. There are food and drinks in the other room. I'll join you all shortly to get acquainted."

Boomer and I step out while the team go to the other room.

"Looks like a great bunch you put together," I say. "Do you think we'll have any more issues with Cowboy?"

Laughing, Boomer says, "Certainly not with Aubrey. She won't hesitate to put him or anyone else in their place. They are a good group, Rip. By the way, it seems as though the DNA report on that mystery body has disappeared. So the investigators are leaving it as it is."

"Well," I say, "they may leave it as it is, but I'm not! Someone killed my lovelies, and I won't stop until I find out who's responsible. Well, I'm thinking that perhaps it would be advisable to start training Rose in self-defense. She always wanted to learn to fight like you. I fear that she could be a target as well, and I can't bear the thought of losing someone else."

Looking into my eyes, Boomer asks, "Are you going to enlighten her of what is going on, that you are alive and well?"

"I'm thinking about it, but I think we need to hit the WarDogs hard and shut them down and try to get answers first," I reply. "What do you think? You still talk to her regularly? Should I stay dead to her?"

"That's up to you, Rip," Boomer replies. "I defend you to her and tell her it's all being investigated and that it's all suspect. In her heart, she knows you didn't do this."

"Well, we have a mission to accomplish first," I reply. "But please, start working with her. I need for her to be okay and able to handle herself."

We walk into the room where the team is socializing. Everyone seems to be hitting it off well, including Ms. Lee. Except Bull. He is just listening and watching. A couple of guys try to converse with him, but he doesn't respond.

Looking at Boomer, I ask, "About what is his story?"

"Well," Boomer replies, "Bull came from Delta Force. He's an expert in just about everything. He's as strong as a bull, and he won't hesitate to rip his enemy's head off with his bare hands, and he's very loyal to his teammates and his mission. He served eight years in prison for involuntary manslaughter when he crushed a man's skull with one hand, when he came upon a guy beating his wife to death in a mall parking lot. He reached down, picking the man up by palming his head and accidentally squeezing too hard, thus killing him. Sentencing him, the judge asked him if he'd ever do that again. His reply was yes, but he'd try not to squeeze so hard next time."

Laughing Boomer adds, "I don't think Bubba gave Bull any sh——t in lockup. It's said that Bull saved a prison guard's life during lockup. An inmate went to shank a guard, and Bull laid out the inmate in one move, disarming him and handing the shank over to the guard. He was well-liked and respected by the guards and the warden."

CHAPTER 3

For the next couple of weeks, we do drills and war games. Sparring and teaching each other our specific talents. We acquire information on strongholds of the WarDogs and where their money as kept and where their heroin kitchens were located and the layouts. Putting together plans to raid them fast and hard before they can alert the other targets. They have three kitchens, all three on opposite ends of town. We plan on hitting all three simultaneously, hitting them deep in their bank.

I want to destroy them completely, but I want answers even more. I want to talk to the top dog. Then I want to kill him with my bare hands. I am going to get answers, even if it kills him.

We have our plans well ready to execute, and we suit up at Boomer's ranch. Our three teams are making last-minute preparations and checking equipment. Aubrey is scouting the top dog and tracking him and his security team. We don't want him at any of the three targets when the raids go down. I want him separate, and I want him to know he is being hunted, make him sweat.

The mission: surprise them, hitting them hard. If they are armed, kill them; if they challenge us, kill them; but watch for the kitchen workers, secure them for the police to deal with. Of course, look for abduction victims, as we knew the WarDogs were heavily involved in kidnapping. Finally, take every penny they have.

Making last-minute preparations. Boomer pulls me aside and says, "Hey, buddy, got a surprise for you, come on."

I follow him out to a shed behind his barn. He opens a lock on the large door, then looks at me. "I went and got your Jeep out of impound, and we've been doing some work on it. You will not recognize it."

He swings the door open.

I stand looking at the front of a mean-looking machine. Flat black with a very roughlike finish. He explains that it's a multicoated tough finish that is bulletproof. It has light bars and night vision or thermal imaging cameras with monitors inside. It even has a 4×4 ground drone with the same night vision or thermal imaging capabilities to spy or watch targets remotely from the vehicle.

"This is very cool, brother," I say. "Thank you. So how is Rose doing?"

"Well, in general, she's doing okay. She misses you terribly and cries, but she's getting better. Her training is coming along well. Peyton is learning also. They both are picking it up very well. Those are two tough little ladies. Peyton is a little powerhouse and is already a force to be reckoned with, and those damn snakes of hers." Boomer shakes his head. "Just what we need, a snake charmer. No wonder Rose would never go to Peyton's house."

I laugh. I then look at Boomer. "Are you ready to do this?"

"Hell, yes, let's do it," he replies.

We return to the team, doing last-minute equipment checks and giving instructions. We split up. Two teams of six are going to hit two houses. The third team of eight of us is going to hit the main warehouse. It has the most security and most likely the biggest cash bank. Each team has a sniper, and all weapons have silencers as not to draw attention in the quiet neighborhoods that these kitchens are in.

Looking over the three teams, I say, "Okay, guys, let's get to our targets, and unless there's a change, 0100, we'll hit them. Leave no one behind. And, gentlemen, don't get dead."

Each team piles into the vehicles and drives off into the night.

We arrive at our target, a mechanics garage by day as a cover. Sniper gets on a roof of a deli across the street. He has a bird's-eye view of two sides of the building and a plain view of their foot soldier they have as a lookout on top of the building. The lookout peers over the edges of the building then walks across to the sides and the back.

Our team stays out of sight as we get a constant update by our eyes across the street. When 0100 comes, we are prepared. Sniper takes out the guard with a single headshot as his gun whispers out its death. We enter the front and the back simultaneously. Guns up at the ready, scanning the rooms as we advance.

I take out two as we enter the second room before they even realize we are there. Hearing other members firing rounds, taking out targets. We enter the kitchen, barking orders at the workers to freeze and put their hands up behind their heads and not move. Covered in dirty lab coats with a mask covering their noses and mouths, they frantically look around for hope of escape.

I watch one worker. He is looking all wild-eyed and in a total panic. He suddenly produces a large knife and lunges at Bull, who isn't even looking his way. Suddenly, Bull's hand shoots up, palming this guy's face, and swiftly drives this guy's head straight through the drywall, snapping his neck. Leaving him to hang there with his head buried in the wall.

Bull grabs the knife out of the man's still-twitching hand and sticks it into his belt. He looks over at me, smiles, and gives me a thumbs-up.

Building secure without a single shot fired by any of them. Quickly we scan the building and find where the money is kept. Didn't have time to count it, but there are at least a couple hundred thousand. Using zip ties, we secure nine workers to each other and around a pole. We are just getting ready to leave when we receive a call from Aubrey.

"Rip," she quietly whispers, "the top dog is coming your way. He's about a block away. Should I delay him until you guys are clear?"

"No," I say. "Let him come."

"Well, he has two bodyguards with him," Aubrey warns. "But he has no idea yet that he's just been robbed."

Giving the sniper on the roof a heads-up. "Don't kill him. When they enter the building, take out the last guy as he enters the door. We'll get the first one and him when they get in the building."

A big dark Caddy SUV pulls up in front. Driver and passenger get out and are looking around with hands in the inside of their jackets. The passenger then opens the back door, and out steps the bastard I want.

As they enter the door, the sniper drops the driver and I shoot the first, leaving my target to fend for himself.

Surprised, he blurts out, "What the f——ck? Who are you?"

I walk up to him face-to-face, fighting back the rage and desire to end his useless life right where he stands, and whisper to him, "I'm your worst nightmare. I'm going to destroy you and your little dog pound piece by piece. And then I'm going to end you, slowly and painfully."

"Well, who are you? What did I do to you?"

"In time," I say. "In time, but until then, you think about your sins. I'll be seeing you again real soon, but here's something for you to remember me by."

Quickly, I bring the gun up and lay the rifle butt across his jaw, breaking it and half of his teeth. He drops to the ground holding his face, screaming in pain.

I kneel beside him, and smiling, I say, "Ouch. That's going to leave a mark, huh?"

We strap him to a pole and quickly leave. the area, heading back to the ranch. The other two teams check in with successful outcomes and are also en route.

Arriving back at the ranch, we gather in the situation room to debrief and to count up the money we confiscated. All three hits go off without a single shot being fired by them.

"Total confirmed kills were thirty-one and forty-three workers captured, and one killed by hand," I say, looking over at Bull.

Bull just looks up from cleaning his gun. He grins, then gives me a thumbs-up and goes back to cleaning. Boomer comes walking in from counting the money and whispers to me, "We took in a total of over $700,000. Not bad for an hour's work."

I look at the guys and say, "You all did very well, and we are going to split up some of this money between you, and the rest will go into the war fund. So you each will receive $10K cash. Not all of our targets are going to be lucrative, and they aren't all going to be this easy. You guys enjoy your evening, you earned it."

The next morning, the news was flooded with what happened. Some commentators were speculating it was a rival gang responsible. The news anchor said there would be a news briefing with the chief of police at 11:00 p.m.

When 11:00 p.m. came, I turned the TV on to see what the chief of police had to say. After stroking his ego, along with the mayor and the other brass in his department, he gave a briefing of the casualties and their story to the public of what happened. Stated it was not a rival gang but what appeared to be a well-trained vigilante group and that it was still under investigation. If anyone had any information, they were to call the hotline on the screen.

"Your identity will remain anonymous," the chief said.

I went out to the barn where Boomer was tending to the horses, and being a horse lover myself, I picked up a brush and began brushing one nearest me, talking and petting him. I filled Boomer in on the news report.

"What's our next move?" he asked.

"Lie low for a week or two, but I want to keep spooking the WarDogs," I said. "I want them jumping at shadows. Each night takes out one member. We need to find out more about their trafficking operation."

Boomer said, "Well, let's talk to Aubrey, see what she knows about it. Aubrey has been a victim of such an operation. Not this particular one, but she can give us some insight. This is what got her into the arts. She vowed to never be a victim again and to do whatever she could to break up these trafficking rings. With our manpower, we could do some damage to their operations."

"Sounds like a plan to me," I said. "We'll talk to her tomorrow."

Then Boomer asked, "So what's after this, Rip? After we destroy the WarDogs, are we going to disband or expand our operation?"

"I've been thinking a lot about that and myself," I said. "I want to keep going. Not just locally but elsewhere too. But that's something we'll need to talk to everyone about. If we do continue, we are going to need a base, a secure compound to work out of. The ranch is great, but it's not secure enough. You have any ideas?"

"I do, actually," Boomer replied. "I think we should put the compound right here on the ranch, Rip."

"I don't know," I replied. "I'm afraid it would draw too much attention and is too easily spotted from the air."

"This is true, if it was above ground." Boomer smiled.

Scratching my chin, deep in thought, I looked at him. "I believe you have something there. Let's talk to the team first and see what they think. After all, we're all in this together. They'll all be here tomorrow. We'll talk to them then. Meantime, Boomer, let's go to the bar."

Boomer looked at me all wide-eyed and surprised. "You're going to talk to Rose?"

"I'm going to play it by ear. You just introduce me as Robert and follow my lead."

We pulled into the bar parking lot, and it looked to be a slow night. I had butterflies in my stomach but was excited at the same time. It had been about seven months since Rip and his family died, and I knew this was not going to be easy. What was Rose's reaction going to be? Would she accept it?

This was all running through my mind as Boomer and I entered the door. I looked around and saw nothing had changed. Looking across the bar, I saw her beautiful smiling face taking care of a customer. We sat at a couple of open stools and waited. She glanced over and saw us and waved and signaled she'd be over in a minute.

Peyton was sitting down from us, and she worked her way over to us. She hugged Boomer and looked at me and said, "And who is this?"

Just then Rose walked up and hugged Boomer. He introduced me to them both as Robert and that I was from out of town visiting.

I politely shook both of their hands as I looked into Rose's eyes. I said, "It's a pleasure to meet you."

She asked what she could get me.

"Captain and Coke please, and do a Fireball with me," I replied.

She stopped and got a strange look on her face. "Do I know you, Robert?"

"I doubt it," I said. "But I've heard plenty about you and Miss Peyton. Boomer talks highly of you both."

Everything in me was screaming to tell her who I was, but I just wasn't comfortable with it yet. Too many loose ends to tie up.

Rose came back with our drinks and shots, and the four of us clinked glasses and down the hatch.

Rose looked at Peyton and asked, "Hey, Peyton, you think you could give me a ride home after work?"

"Of course," Peyton replied. "Where's your car?"

"It wouldn't start, had to get a ride in. The damn car has been costing way more than it's worth lately. I've got to get another one soon. I'm over it. Going to have to try to put in extra hours or get a second job. As if I don't have my plate full already."

She looked down, the beautiful smile disappearing from her face, and she looked up at Boomer. With tears filling her eyes, she said, "Damn it, Boomer, I miss him more and more every day. Why did this have to happen? I go out to the cemetery at least once a week, and I sit and talk to him as if he was there, but…"

She started to cry. "He doesn't answer me. I keep expecting him to answer me. I guess in a way he does. I know and can hear him in my head what I know he'd say. I just pray that this pain goes away soon."

Fighting back the tears myself. Seeing her pain was killing me.

Peyton went to Rose and held her tight. She too had tears running down her face.

Awkwardly, I spoke up. "You know the cliché, as long as one is in your heart, then they still live on. I know it's not the same as the physical presence, but it's all we've got."

"Did you know Rip?" Rose asked.

"Yes, I knew him very well," I replied. "We served together. Let's have another shot."

As Rose got four more shots lined up, Boomer looked at me. "I'm guessing you're not saying anything today?"

Rose came with the shots, and we toasted friendships and Rip. We all downed the shots, and I told Boomer, "Time to go, buddy, we've got work to do."

The three exchanged hugs as I headed to the door.

Rose yelled after me, "Hold on there, Robert! You're not getting away that easy." She came up and hugged me close, saying, "You're part of this now. Any friend of Rip and Boomer is a friend of mine."

I coldly returned the hug, afraid that if I gave her my normal full warm hug I'd give away who I was. Besides, emotionally I might be broken, and this is no time to show the weakness in my armor that only Rose was capable of piercing.

When we got back to the ranch, the team was already there and waiting for us. Aubrey looked at us and said, "You two out drinking while we sit here waiting for you." Then she looked straight into my eyes and asked, "How's Rose? Did you tell her who you were?"

Caught by surprise, I looked at Boomer. "Do they know?"

Aubrey chimed in as Boomer was looking dumbfounded, "Yes, we know. Boomer didn't say anything, I overheard your conversation out in the barn earlier."

Looking around at the guys as they half-encircled us, Aubrey said, "We're all behind you. We're a team, we're a family. Always. And we already voted on what we want to do after we finish with the WarDogs. We want to go kick ass whenever and wherever that takes us. Our judicial system is broken."

"So then you all agree that we should establish a base for operations here?" I asked.

Everyone's hands went up, and yeses were spoken up around the room.

"So be it," I said. "Make it so number one." I looked at Boomer.

Aubrey came up to me and gave me a big hug. She looked into my eyes and said, "Thank you for allowing me to be part of this. I feel like this is where I belong."

Each man came up one at a time and shook our hands and exchanged our appreciation. The last one to come up was Bull, looking all stone-faced serious. He looked down at me, and for the first time, he spoke. "Thank you, Rip. I've got your back, brother."

He gave me a thumbs-up and what I think might have been a smile, but it looked more like he was baring his teeth in a growl.

I shook his massive hand and replied, "And I have yours, my friend."

Pulling off Aubrey to the side, I said, "Okay, can you get me some information on this a——hole? I want to know where he goes and what he does and when. It's time to have a nice chat with him. I want answers, and then it's time to close his book. I want to get him out alone where he has no resources to help him."

"Give me a couple of days, Rip," she replied.

"Please be careful, Aubrey. We need you."

Her little face lit up, and she smiled the biggest smile from ear to ear. "I'll get started right away if you are done with me here?"

"The sooner, the better," I said.

With that, Aubrey slipped out into the night and was gone.

After some time, we discussed our plans as a group on just how we were going to establish this secure home base and where we determined that it would be underground, and we would use overseas shipping containers as the primary structure. Arranged in a layout forming walls and bridging the containers, leaving caverns for vehicle storage, armory, living quarters, courtyards, storage, a control center, with a series of tunnels. Two tunnels that we can drive vehicles through and about six-man tunnels branching out in multiple directions, coming out in various places such as the house basement, the barn, the feed shed, out in the woods into fake tree stumps.

All entrances electronically locked and monitored from the control room. The whole complex would be encased in at least three-foot concrete walls poured around the structure once assembled. and it'll be under a new machine shed that Boomer would be able to park his farm equipment in. Between the whole team, we have the expertise to do this without any outside contractors.

After a few days, Aubrey came to me with a wealth of information. "I followed him, and I've stumbled on a warehouse where he has kids and young women confined, Rip. It's pretty secure, but I managed to get in and overheard a conversation that they are going to be shipped out east to a marina, transferred to a boat, and taken to some island.

"Rip." Aubrey looked at me. "I've heard of this island, but I don't know where it's at. It's a pleasure island for high-ranking officials of governments from all over the world, celebrities, athletes, and wealthy tycoons. They go there and have sex with little kids. It gets secretly recorded and filed, then it's used to blackmail these perverts. Sway government policies, and it's all at the expense of these children's lives. They are brutally abused, tortured, and murdered. Some are sold to slavery all over the world for these sick bastards' pleasure."

I listened to this in disbelief, feeling sick to my stomach. Aubrey, now showing emotions, recounted what could have been her fate, knowing this was a whole underground operation so large and corrupt.

Boomer spoke up as he approached us. "What the hell are we going to do, Rip? This is huge. We aren't big enough to do anything with this island."

Deep in thought, I said, "Well, we may not be prepared to tackle this island yet, but I do know this is one shipment of children that are not going to be taken there. Aubrey, how many kids do you estimate are there right now?"

"I don't know, Rip," Aubrey answered. "I'd estimate at least a couple dozen."

"How are they paid for?" I asked.

"So much per head, just like cattle, going by their ages and also their attractiveness. Pictures are sent of each one, and then the money is sent to the captors' account, and when the deposit is verified, the shipment is sent."

"What happens if the WarDogs receive the money and these people don't get their shipment?" I asked.

Aubrey said, "Then sweepers are sent, and they wipe out the entire organization—in this case, the WarDogs. These people are not to be screwed with, and they will not be stolen from."

"Well then, we need to get prepared for this operation," I said. "But first, I have a score to settle with this bastard." I turned to Audrey. "When are these kids being shipped?"

"Friday night," Aubrey said.

"Okay," I said. "After they verify the payment Friday, I'll go after the top dog while the rest of the team will go after the warehouse to rescue these kids. Aubrey, work with Boomer and give him the layout of this warehouse so the team can prepare. First, talk to me: where's the best place for me to settle the score with this animal?"

We had a little over two days to prepare, from what information we had. This WarDog operation was huge and well-fortified. The lives of a couple of dozen children are depending on our success. Boomer and I worked with the team. We gathered resources and acquired vehicles needed for penetration of the perimeter barriers. We borrowed a couple of state dump trucks with plows to use as armored personnel carriers to break through the perimeter and carry guys through to the interior.

Aubrey would take out the two WarDogs lookouts quickly and quietly first. One unit would locate and secure the children until the other units would finish mopping up the rest of the compound. The whole operation should take less than five minutes. Once everyone was exterminated, Aubrey would stay behind as a safety barrier and keep the kids calm until the police arrive, and then she would disappear into the night. Meantime, I would be stalking my prey elsewhere.

Friday came, and it was nearing time to execute our operation. One team member was monitoring the WarDogs' account to watch for the payoff and prepare to transfer it to a money-laundering account so as we may acquire the funds ourselves. That would also signal us when the transfer of these children would start, then our operation would begin.

I was tracking my prey for the meantime, waiting for my chance to have my chat with him. Aubrey had informed me that he had a girl he would frequently go see out in the country. That was what I was waiting for.

Dressed in a black tactical uniform, I used the shadows as cover and watched as he left his house with two of his bodyguards. I received a message that the payment had been made and the operation was going to begin.

I straddled the motorcycle and fell in behind my prey's car as they drove off, and as I had hoped, they were heading out of town. I stayed back, barely out of sight to not arouse attention to me. We got out on to roads I remembered from when we used to go for country drives with Crystal and the girls. Bringing up those beautiful memories from another lifetime. With these sweet memories also came the rage of what this bastard took from me. It was time for justice!

I twisted the throttle and gained on my prey with revenge filling my soul. I approached the car. They had been watching and began to accelerate. I pulled out my .45. I was going to have to shoot out the tires.

Just then one of the bodyguards stuck his arm and part of his torso out of the window and fired a couple of shots at me. I fired back, forcing him back into the vehicle. I fired a second shot, blowing out his rear tire. The car began slowing down quickly to a stop as I laid the bike down off the road, separating myself from it as I disappeared into the night and the brush. This was my territory, my domain.

The car had come to a stop as I watched both bodyguards quickly exit the car with guns drawn and taking cover the best. They couldn't know where I was. My target exited and got into a prone position for cover. The one shooter sprayed wildly into the brush in hopes I'd get hit. Unfortunately for him, I was behind him, and I fired one shot to the back of his head, thus eliminating where his face used to be.

Quickly I relocated as to avoid fire from the second shooter, as he turned and fired wildly in the direction I had been. Again, I popped up behind him and fired a round into his head like I did the first shooter, his face exploding into a bloody mess. My prey was now in panic mode got up and ran into the brush.

The hunt was on, but I could hear him as he fumbled and tripped over himself multiple times. I followed him quietly as I flanked him. He occasionally fired around behind him, thinking I was behind him. I yelled to him, allowing my voice to carry, throwing him off on my location. He would fire where he thought my voice came from.

"You're not such a badass without your boys, are you?" I said. "Do you know you're going to die a slow, horrible death tonight?"

"Who are you!" he yelled.

I came out of the darkness like lightning. With my knife, I cut deeply into his thigh and disappeared back into the night. He screamed in pain, firing several rounds in the direction I had disappeared.

I laughed out loud, mocking him. "Come on, you can do better than that. Or do you only like hunting defenseless children?"

I threw a knife at his gun hand. The knife stuck through his wrist, rendering that hand useless. Dropping his gun, he quickly grabbed it with his good hand, firing a couple of rounds where I had been. A second knife found its target on his other wrist. Now he was on the ground, screaming in pain and cursing the maker whom he would soon meet.

I casually walked out of the darkness and approached him.

He squinted at me, asking why. "Why are you doing this, and who are you? I don't know you!"

"Yes, a——hole, you know me," I said. "You put a hit out on my family. You murdered my family!"

His eyes widened as the realization hit him. "But...but you're dead!"

"No, a——hole, I'm alive and well, but my babies are dead! Who was the fourth person in that fire?"

"I don't know!" he screamed. "I thought it was you. There were only three of them there when the hit took place." He was now slobbering and panting as he was losing blood quickly. "We thought you showed up after and tried to rescue them from the fire and got engulfed in the flames. I don't know who it was, I swear to God!"

"Well, you can swear to him personally," I whispered, as I drove my knife through his neck and up into his skull.

His body stiffened. He gurgled his last breath, and he went limp as his eyes, wide with horror, stared blankly to the skies.

Meantime, back at the ranch, the team had completed the operation. We had a couple of injuries but nothing serious. I arrived at a happy group of great guys and a gal. Talked about the operation and how great it felt to rescue these children. To see the relief in their little faces when they realized they were going to go home.

Cowboy bragged about Aubrey, recalling him watching her scaling walls like a spider, throwing stars, taking out targets, and showing no mercy whatsoever. Aubrey turning all red-faced when everyone was praising her.

Cowboy looked at her and said, "You look good in red."

Their eyes locked for a second. She was smiling as she approached him. In a reflex, he covered his throat as she reached up and smacked him in the head. Everyone began laughing at Cowboy as she turned and walked away.

Boomer saw me watching and approached me and said, "Well?"

"It's over, Boomer, but the plot thickens," I said. "He didn't know who the fourth person was. He said they thought it was me. They did kill the girls and Crystal, but that's all. He swore to God."

"And?" he asked.

"And now he's dead and the WarDogs are done. How did the operation go?" I asked.

"Well, we killed almost everyone except one."

"Except one?" I asked.

"Yes," Boomer replied. "It seems as though the FBI had an undercover agent working for this group."

"Oh?" I asked.

"Yes, he identified himself as we were going through the trash. He even took out a couple of shooters for us. We left him with the kids until the police arrived. Aubrey stayed behind in the shadows just in case he wasn't who he said he was. When the police arrived, he identified himself to them, and his identity was verified."

"Interesting," I said. "Did you get a name?"

"Special Agent Blye," Boomer said. "He asked us who we were when we were done. I just said we're just American patriots that are tired of this trash getting away with murder. He wasn't too happy about us interfering and forcing him to blow his cover. Like I told him, your cover is only blown if there was anyone left alive to blow the whistle. There isn't."

"Then we were a success. How did we do with their account? Did we get the money from them?"

"Yes, we got a little over two million dollars with what was paid for the kids and what was already in the account, we just cleaned them out."

"Great," I said. "Take a million and split it among everyone. Take the rest and put it in the war chest."

CHAPTER 4

The next day, I went birthday shopping for Rose. I decided that was when I was going to fill her in on everything. She'll either love me or hate me, but either way, I couldn't keep going like this without my best friend. I could only pray that she'll understand.

The entire team pitched in for a major gift for her, and I was humbled by their generosity. They all wanted to be a part of the surprise and the reveal. So about a week later, I got the call I was waiting for, and I took Aubrey with me to pick it up. She was more excited about it than I was, I think. We pulled into the paint shop and walked into the door and gave the man my name, Robert Polin.

He said, "Yes, sir, it's all ready for you. I'd imagine you want to see it first before you give it to the little lady." He looked at Aubrey.

"Yes, we do want to see it, and no, it's not for her," I replied.

"Oh, okay, follow me," he said, leading us into the shop.

There it sat: a brand-new Jeep Wrangler. Painted in pink-and-gray camouflage. It was lifted about three inches. Big 35s mudders mounted on black custom wheels. Aftermarket steel bumpers and a winch. The interior was trimmed in black and pink. Black seat covers with a single pink rose embroidered in the backrest. It had a matching gray soft top.

"What do you think, Aubrey?" I asked. "Do you think she'll like it?"

"Well, if she doesn't, then I'll take it," she replied.

I looked at the mechanic and said, "It looks great. We'll take it."

Aubrey drove the Jeep back to the ranch. The rest of the team was there waiting when we pulled in.

Boomer was delighted, and asked, "When are we giving it to her, Rip?"

"Tonight, Boomer, tonight." I smiled.

Each man on the team crawled into the Jeep with a pen of paint and signed their names someplace on the interior. I was the last one, and I signed it on the windshield frame just above the sun visor: "Friends forever. Love you. Rip."

Boomer and I pulled into the parking lot. Not a very-busy-looking night. Yet. It was about to get really busy when the rest of the team shows up in about a half hour bringing the Jeep with them. We walked in and were greeted with Rose's sweet smile and hug. We ordered our drinks, and I asked for shots all around.

When all the shots were given out, Boomer said, "To sweet Rose, happy birthday!"

"You remembered!" Rose exclaimed. "Thank you, Boomer. The surprises keep coming."

"What do you mean?" I asked.

"I went to pay some bills today to find out they've already been paid," she replied. "As it turns out, all my bills are paid, including my rent. Plus, I found a $200 gift card for groceries in my mailbox." She looked at Boomer. "Did you do this? You know Rip used to do this every year for my birthday."

"I don't know anything about that, Rose," Boomer said. "My gift to you is coming later." He laughed.

Rose stood there, trying to figure out who it could have been. "Has to be someone that knew Rip," she said, as she rubbed her neck.

I motioned for Rose to come over to me, and I spun her around to massage her neck—her beautiful neck. I knew exactly where her pain was, and I went straight to it, massaging the knots out. She had her head down a little bit and said, "Oh my god, that's the spot."

Suddenly, she stiffened up and pulled away, turning and looking at us with tears filling her eyes. "What's going on?" she said sternly. "Boomer, you know something. What are you up to? First, my bills get paid, like Rip used to do. You order Fireball shots to toast my birthday, like Rip used to do, and now"—she looked into my eyes—"you know exactly where my injury is in my neck and go straight to it."

Tears were now running down her perfect little face.

I looked at Boomer and said, "It's time."

Boomer looked at Peyton. "Can you watch the bar for Rose for a few minutes?"

"What is going on?" Peyton said in concern for her friend.

"I'll fill you in later," Boomer replied. "Let's go out to the patio, Rose."

Rose led the way outside, b——tching at us. "I don't know what kind of sh——t you two are trying to pull here, but it's sick, just sick, and I won't stand for it." She stopped and squared off with us face-to-face.

"What the hell is going on?" she blurted out.

"Please calm down, Rose, it'll be fine," I said, trying to reassure her. "Rose, remember when you asked me if we've met before the day I came in?"

Nodding her head yes, she nervously acknowledged that day.

"Well, the fact of the matter is, Rose, the answer is yes, we have met before."

Rose stopped breathing and, studying my eyes, she asked, "Where? Where do we know each other from, and what the hell does it have to do with all of this?"

"Rose," I said, "I am Rip."

She froze for a second. She then looked at Boomer, then back at me. "What? What did you just say? Because I'm pretty sure I just heard you telling me that you are Rip, my best friend that I lost in a fire last year, that we buried." She looked again at Boomer for assurance and back at me. "You are a sick son of a b——tch, Robert!"

The next thing I knew, I got b——tch-slapped into next week, knocking me off balance. Rose repositioned herself into a fighting stance and was fully ready to take me on.

I looked back at her red face and beautiful tear-filled eyes and said, "I certainly deserved that." Looked at Boomer, who was standing there, chuckling, with his hand up over his mouth.

Boomer said, "Damn, Rip, you didn't even see that coming. Should I get the team together for a search party? Because I'm pretty sure she just knocked you into next week somewhere." He looked back at Rose. Her eyes were now wide and tears were pouring down her face.

"I'm confused," she managed to say. "Boomer, is this Rip? Do not lie to me!"

Boomer and Rose locked eyes, and the smile were gone from his face.

"Yes, Rose, this is Rip," Boomer said. "Happy birthday."

I looked at Rose and said, "I love you, Rose, forever in a day." I handed her the now-dried-up black rose that she had placed on my casket last year.

The strong woman whom I've always admired was now weary and shaking from head to toe as she looked at me, and the reality of who I was setting in.

"Rip!" she yelled, and dove into my arms trembling and crying uncontrollably.

I wrapped my arms around her and held her tight as she now was off the ground and her legs were wrapped around me.

"Why did you do this to me? Why do you not look like Rip? What the hell happened?" Wanting answers, she slowly unwrapped her leg hold on to me, still holding me with her arms but studying my face.

Not being able to hold back my tears, I looked back into her bright blue and bloodshot eyes. I said, "We'll explain everything."

"You know," she said, "this is an improvement over your other mug." She laughed.

Boomer erupted into laughter, saying, "That's exactly what I told him when the doctor was taking the bandages off."

Looking like she was feeling a little wobbly, Rose was chuckling now, and she stepped back and sat down. Looking back up at us, she asked, "Is this a dream? Is this real?"

I sat beside her and took her by the hands and looked into her eyes. "I've missed you so much. Boomer is my best friend and teammate, and he's been great. But you, you are everything. I think of you every day, longing to have you back in my life to complete me."

Tears started to flow down my face. "My babies are gone, Rose. They're gone, and it's my fault. My heart is shattered, and my life is gone. Rip is dead to the world, and only a few can ever know who Robert really is."

Suddenly, we're aware of someone else behind us. I looked, and there stood Peyton, with wide eyes and tears and her jaw half-open. I stood up and faced her.

"She's right," she said. "That *is* an improvement." She approached me with open arms.

I opened my arms to her and got punched in the gut.

"How dare you do this to her? Or me, for that matter."

Boomer was dying laughing now. Looking at Peyton, he said, "That was perfectly executed and in perfect form."

Everyone was now laughing, and I joined in once I got my breath back.

"Hey, Rose," Peyton said. "I came out to tell you we are getting swamped all a sudden. I need help."

"Oh, okay," Rose said, getting up and trying to fix herself.

We all walked into a full bar, filled with the regulars and my whole team, and they all erupted into singing "Happy Birthday." Each one came up to Rose face-to-face and shook her hand and introduced themselves.

Aubrey worked her way to Rose wearing a pink-and-gray camo hoodie a couple of sizes too big for her. She hugged Rose and introduced herself and took the hoodie off, handing it to Rose.

"This is yours," she said. "I think we need to go outside."

The whole team now standing behind Aubrey, agreeing with her. Rose, being all confused, looked at me with a questioning look.

I laughed and said, "No, you don't know these people, but you will. This is my team. Let's go outside."

I helped Rose with her hoodie as we headed for the parking lot. The door opened, and there parked right at the door was her Jeep. A dozen pink and black roses fixed in a vase sat on the hood, and a small banner hung across the grill, saying, "Happy birthday, Rose."

Rose froze and looked in disbelief. Everyone was laughing at the look on her face.

Totally bewildered, she chokingly asked, "This is mine?" She looked at me. "Did you?"

Chuckling, I replied, "No, it was a team effort."

Her eyes, now wide and amazed, looked across all the smiling faces of her new friends, as they were high-fiving each other. She worked her way to the Jeep, looking and touching. Looking inside, she was overwhelmed with unspeakable joy.

"Oh my god, what a day," she blurted out.

Aubrey handed her the keys and opened the door for her, pointing out the multiple signatures of the whole team.

Rose looked at everyone and said, "I am lost for words."

One at a time, she went to each and hugged them tight, thanking them until she got to Bull. She froze, looking up at his stone face looking down at her. She reached up with both hands and took his face and pulled him down to her level, looking into his black eyes, then she planted a warm kiss on his cheek.

Bull slowly stood up, and for the first time, we saw a light in his eyes as he broke into the biggest smile we've ever seen.

Everyone cheered, saying, "BULL, BULL, BULL!"

Rose just stood smiling and was so incredibly happy.

CHAPTER 5

Meantime, back at the ranch, the team is preparing to break ground for the subterranean base. Plans are laid out in the toolshed, and equipment is arriving and being unloaded. Cowboy is acting job foreman, and he's discussing with the operators what he expects. The rest of the team are gathered around, listening and offering their assistance according to their knowledge.

Boomer pulls in and is getting out of his Hummer. He's impressed by the teamwork among the guys as he approaches me. We bumped fists as he asks, "Are you ready for this new adventure?"

"Yes," I replied. "Let's do this. Where have you been?"

"Oh, I was in town working with Peyton and Rose, finished filling them in on what has been going on," Boomer says.

"I see. Yes, I'll be getting together with Rose later and having a real conversation with her. How did she take the briefing?" I asked.

"She was a little upset, mainly because we didn't enlighten her earlier. But she understands that it was for her protection. I'll tell you, Rip, I haven't seen her this happy in a long time."

"Good," I said. "She deserves the best. I love you, brother. Thank you for being there for me through this and for Rose too. I know it had to be tough. I appreciate you." I hugged him as Cowboy approached us.

"Okay, okay, you all need to go get a room." Cowboy shook his head. "Next thing you know, you two are going to get matching tattoos or man buns or something."

We chuckled and turned to him.

"Are we ready to break ground?" I asked.

"Yes, Sir Rip," Cowboy replied. "The shovels are ready."

Just then Rose's Jeep comes down the drive. She and Peyton get out, and Peyton says, "Let's get this party started."

We walk to the site, and Cowboy hands Boomer and me shovels, as the team gathers in front of us.

"Ladies and gentlemen," I said. "First, I want to thank you for joining us on this journey that we are about to embark on. Each one of you is extraordinary. I've never worked with such an amazing group outside of the teams. We've come together from various backgrounds and specialties, and we've done some serious ass-kicking. We are not looked upon kindly by authorities, and the public probably has mixed emotions about vigilantes running around town. But if we don't do what we do, it's just going to get worse.

"We saved the lives of a couple of dozen innocent children, and there are so many more out there waiting for a miracle. Approximately eight hundred thousand children are missing just in the United States alone every year. Not all are abducted, but a large percentage of them are."

I looked over at Aubrey. "And we have here someone that's been there, and she's spearheading this effort to make a difference. She has connections in the underground and the missing and exploited children center. So we are going to build this heavily fortified bunker to work out of as our safe zone. When we're not going after these traffickers, we'll be going after other things like meth or heroin kitchens, gangs, terrorists, punk asses that slip through the cracks of justice. So, let's get started."

Boomer and I grabbed the shovels and put the tips to the ground and simultaneously stepped on the shovels, driving them into the ground. Pictures were taken for prosperity. Everyone clapped and whistled.

Cowboy yelled out, "Okay, gentlemen! Start your engines, and let's dig this hole."

I turned to Rose and Peyton and gave them both hugs and said, "I'm so glad that you two are here and part of this." Turning to Rose,

I said, "Thank you for being you and understanding. I'm sorry for any pain I've caused you."

They looked at each other then back at me and Peyton said, "And we're sorry for hurting you."

They began laughing. I laughed with them and hugged and kissed them both.

Looking at Rose, I asked, "Are you ready to go out for a drive and go down to the lake?"

With a smile, she replied, "Yes, I am. Let's go."

We turned to leave and walked to my Jeep, passing Aubrey on the way. Aubrey smiled and winked, hugged Rose, and gave me a hug, whispering to me, "All set."

We had the top down and the doors off to enjoy the beautiful weather as we drove through the countryside. The sun was bright and warm. I glanced at my stunning Rose, the sun shining through her coal-black hair as it blew in the wind. And that smile—that smile that I've missed for almost a year but seemed like an eternity.

The sun was setting as we arrived at the lake. We sat in silence on the dam and watched the beauty as the sun sank and sparkled across the water. We then drove around to the woods on the lake and walked down the slope, where little tiki torches were burning around a blanket and there was a bottle of wine in a bucket of ice with a couple of glasses.

Rose looked at me, questioning, "How did you do this?"

I laughed and looked out into the woods and yelled, "Thank you, Aubrey!"

Rose was looking around for her.

Then I yelled, "You can go now!"

There was silence for a minute, then in the distance, we heard Aubrey's sweet voice reply, "Okay, okay, I'm leaving. Love you, guys."

"We love you too," I replied.

I was a bit nervous as was Rose, judging by the quiver in her voice. This was the first time we've been alone since last year, and so much had happened. So many changes.

We talked about little things at first, just catching up. I opened the bottle of wine and poured us a couple of glasses as we sat on the blanket. I turned to her and looked into her blue eyes as they glistened from the candlelight. We raised our glasses.

I said, "To the best friend and companion any man could ever need or want in his life. The yin to my yang. You complete me, Rose. I love you."

Her little face smiled up at me as she replied with a sigh. "I love you too."

Slowly I bent down and gently held her chin and jaw with my fingers and tenderly kissed her perfect lips. Our very first kiss.

Just then the sky erupted into a flurry of fireworks. We both began chuckling, our foreheads pressed together.

"We are never going to have privacy," I stated.

I put my hand behind her neck and kissed her forehead and yelled into the woods, "Aubrey, you little sh——t!"

Then we heard a giggle and a reply. "It's not Aubrey!"

I looked at Rose questioningly.

Rose cracked up, saying, "It's Peyton. You aren't the only one that can be sneaky."

Rose yelled, "Thank you, honey! See you later, and don't wreck my Jeep."

We heard a burst of laughter, and she was gone.

Rose looked at me in the eye. "I'm the yin to your yang."

We talked for hours, heart to heart. We cried, and we laughed. She held me close, and I melted like butter. It was a beautiful evening at the lake.

The sun came up. We were cuddled together under a blanket, me lying on my back and Rose wrapped around me, her head nestled in my neck as I listened to her soft breathing. My hand gently ran through her long hair. I gently kissed her forehead. "Good morning, beautiful. We need to get home."

We gathered up everything and headed back to the Jeep to find hot coffee in the cupholders: one labeled Rose and the other labeled Other. Giggling to ourselves, we got into the Jeep and headed back to the ranch.

We pulled in to find the team already at work. Boomer greeted us with that ornery smile, hugging Rose.

"What's going on, buddy?" I asked.

"These guys have been at it since about 0400 this morning," Boomer said. "They are making good time."

"That's great," I said. "We have a couple of shipping containers coming today. Do we have the Cosmoline to start painting the containers?"

"Yes, we do, and we have a couple of guys ready to start as soon as the containers get here. By the way, Rip, we have some information on a heroin kitchen in town we need to check out as soon as possible."

"Okay," I said. "I'll go check it out tonight. Aubrey has family stuff to do today, so I'll take care of it." Looking at Rose, I asked, "Do you want to drive me tonight? All you have to do is drop me off and go away until I call for you to pick me up. Shouldn't take too long."

"I have to work tonight, what time are you thinking?" she asked.

"Right after you close the bar," I replied. "I'll pick you up."

"Okay," Rose replied. "I've got to run. Got errands to run, so I'll talk to you in a little while."

She walked up to me and wrapped her arms around me, looking up at me. She said, "I had a great time at the lake. Thank you."

"The pleasure was all mine," I said.

I kissed her, and she turned and walked away.

That night, I went to the bar to pick up Rose. I texted her to let her know I was waiting outside for her. I didn't want to go in as I was dressed out in black tactical.

She came out, locking the door behind her, and got in the driver's door. Looking at me, she asked, "Where to?" She greeted me with a hug and a gentle hand squeeze.

I gave her directions as we drove off, and I was applying black camouflage on my face. We got into the quiet neighborhood, and I pointed out a dark area where she could let me out. Threw the switch for the interior lights so they wouldn't come on when I opened the door.

Just as I was getting ready to open the door, I looked down the block, and at the end of the street I could see an orange glow flickering. Realizing that it was a fire and there was not one person in sight. This house was burning, and no one knew it.

I looked at Rose and said, "You stay right here because it's about to get crazy, and I'm going to need to make a quick escape."

I got out and ran down the street to the fire. As I got close, I could see that the upper level was engulfed in flames and there were lights on downstairs. I yelled "Fire!" and for someone to call 911 a couple of times, then ran to the front door and tried to open it. It was locked, but I could see someone moving around inside. I kicked the door open and ran into the house. She was a short chunky lady standing at the kitchen sink doing dishes, and I scared the hell out of her.

I told her, "Ma'am, you need to get out of this house, it's on fire. Is there anyone else here?"

Now terrified, she looked at me and said, "This is a triplex. There's an apartment beside me and one upstairs!"

"Okay," I said. "You get out of here now! I'll check out the other two apartments."

I ran next door and kicked in their door also. There was a couple in bed sound asleep, even after the noise of me kicking in their door. I woke them up and told them to get out. Then I ran outside because the entrance to the upstairs was from the outside. By now, several neighbors were outside, assisting the people coming out of the house.

I ran up the stairs to the door. There was a wisp of smoke coming out from under the door.

This is bad, I thought to myself, remembering my firefighting training.

I reached up for the doorknob, and it was hot. I felt the door itself, and it too was hot. Just then I saw the door paint start to blister. I took off running down the stairs as fast as I could, just as the door exploded open and flames shot out and down the stairs behind me. It was too late for anyone who would have been up there.

The neighbors were now looking at me for what they should do. In the distance, I could hear the sirens coming and knew that I had to disappear before the police arrived, as I knew they would want to know who I was and what I was doing in black tactical with an AR slung over my shoulder.

One neighbor had his garden hose out, trying to squirt out the fire. The flames now were burning high and hot, so the small stream of water was evaporating before it even hit the flames. He was afraid his house was going to catch on fire. I told him he wasn't doing any good.

I pointed to his house, telling him, "The only chance you have is to try to spray your house and try to keep it cool as much as possible."

I called for Rose and told her to drive around the corner from me out of sight and that I'll meet her there. The sirens were awfully close, and I made a fast exit, leaving everyone to fend for themselves. I ran around the corner, and there was Rose waiting for me. I jumped into the Jeep, and we got out of there, passing the patrol cars and fire trucks coming on the scene.

Rose was excited and flustered, not being used to this kind of adrenaline rush. "Oh my god, Rip, are you insane? You ran right into that burning house. I was scared to death. Damn it, Rip, don't do that to me. I lost you once. I can't be losing you again! I should beat the sh——t out of you!"

I turned to her and chuckled and said, "Rose, Rose, don't threaten me with a good time."

She looked at me with fire shooting from those teared-up baby blues. "You a——hole," she blurted out, as she playfully punched me in the chest. She smiled.

I told her, "We may as well call it a night and try again in a day or two, when things calm down. I'm sure they'll be on the lookout for suspicious people in that neighborhood."

The next morning, the newspaper had the story on the fire. The couple in the apartment upstairs had fallen asleep, and a cigarette caught the bed on fire, killing both. It also stated that multiple witnesses had seen a heavily armed man in black alert the neighbors and had saved the three people in the lower apartments. They hailed him as a hero and asked for him to come forward for recognition.

I shook my head. *Isn't going to happen*, I thought to myself.

Though I was glad the three survivors made it out safely, I felt bad that I couldn't save the couple upstairs.

* * *

There was mass confusion and fire everywhere. Soldiers screaming orders, other soldiers carrying the wounded and equipment from the burning HS53 Super Stallions. From in the fire, I could hear my teammates screaming for help as I tried to approach them through the flames. The heat was so intense my uniform began smoldering, and every exposed hair on my body was burning.

Through the flames, I could see one of the door gunners looking back at me, screaming, as his uniform was now burning. He was trapped in the burning wreckage, screaming for me to shoot him and that he didn't want to die this way. I still pushed to get to him, but the heat was just too intense. I could not get myself to shoot him. I reached for him just as my uniform sleeve burst into flames. I pulled back, extinguishing my sleeve, just as something in the wreckage exploded, throwing me backward, silencing the screams from the wreckage.

Just then I woke up in a panic, sweating and yelling, jumping out of bed, looking around, realizing it was a posttraumatic nightmare. Poor Rose was scared out of her mind as she jumped out of bed away from me, not knowing what was going on. I quickly regathered my composure and reassured her it was okay.

I was still shaking and breathing hard. Rose went into the bathroom and got a cold wet washcloth to wipe me down and soothe me, as I explained to her for the first time what had taken place many years before. I explained to her that occasionally something would trigger these nightmares. It could be a sight, sound, smell, or an event. In this case, it was probably the house fire.

She sat on the bed beside me with her arm around me, looking at me, and she asked, "Are you okay?"

I assured her I was fine, as she gently kissed my forehead. We laid back down and had small talk until we both were ready to go back to sleep, facing each other, holding hands, and drifting off.

The next morning, I woke up and watched her sleep for a minute, in awe of this angel. Wondering how I could be so lucky to be so blessed.

I slipped into the kitchen and made her a cup of coffee the way she likes it, putting it in a tumbler to keep it hot for her. Wrote her a note, picked a fresh rose from the bush outside the house, and put it all on the nightstand beside the bed. Then I slipped out the door to go see the team as they were at work on the site.

CHAPTER 6

Boomer approached me as I was looking over the progress. The mammoth hole in the ground was taking shape nicely.

Boomer greeted me with a fist bump and said, "Cowboy says that the digging for the compound is almost complete, and we'll start putting in the drainage, septic, and piping by tomorrow morning, then bring in the gravel."

"That's great," I said. "We're ahead of schedule by at least a week."

Boomer agreed. "Yes, these guys are great. Cowboy has them working around the clock in shifts. Hey, by the way, our IT guy Neil is having an issue. I think we need to address it."

Looking around the site, he spots Neil and whistles for him. Neil, though being one of the team, is small in stature and somewhat frail-looking. He approaches us, reaching, out shaking our hands.

"So, what's going on, Neil?" I asked.

Neil, rather feeblish, replied, "I have a daughter in the hospital. Her boyfriend put her there. I've warned him on multiple occasions to keep his hands off of her or else." Briefly looking at himself, saying, "Look at me. I'm not very intimidating. He just looks at me and blows me off."

"Well, listen to me, Neil," I said. "We are family here. Your daughter is our daughter too, and we won't tolerate this. Has she tried to leave him?"

44

"Yes," Neil said. "But he hunts her down and hounds her until she gives in to his threats."

"Well, we will have to have a little chat, maybe a small attitude adjustment," I said. "How does that sound to you, Neil? You let Boomer know where he works at, and we'll send Bull down to, shall we say, pick him up and bring him to us to introduce him to the family."

"Oh sh——t." Neil chuckled.

I yelled for Bull and a couple of other guys. As they approached, I looked at Bull and said, "Hey, Uncle Bull, we need you to go pick up this little a——hole and bring him to that abandoned garage down by that little lake by the plaza. We are going to feed some fish. This a——hole seems to think he can beat on a member of our family and ignore warnings. Bull, take the van, and we'll meet you there in a little while."

About an hour later, the van pulls up outside the garage. Bull gets out and slides open the side door of the van, reaches in, and grabs this guy who is unconscious and with both hands and feet. He carries him like luggage into the garage, where we waited. Threw a rope over a rafter and tied it to his hands, hoisting him into the air, dangling. Wrapped a heavy log chain around his feet and placed a big bucket of quick cement on the ground, putting his feet in it.

We stood around the guy, waiting for him to wake up.

Looking at Bull, I asked him, "You didn't kill him, did you?"

Without a word, Bull opened his water bottle and splashed it on the guy's face.

Neil, smiling from ear to ear, says, "Wakey-wakey, a——hole."

Groggy, the guy lifted his head, sputtering water. Looked around at the situation he was in.

"What the hell is going on?" he asked nervously, looking down and seeing his feet drying in cement.

Neil walked up to him and smugly asked him, "Did I not tell you to never hit my daughter again or else? Did you think that I was just joking with you? How many times did I warn you? Well, now you can deal with the family. Can you swim, a——hole?"

One of the guys opened the garage door so he could see the lake outside the door.

He began fighting against the rope, trying to get down.

Neil looked up at him and said, "Now you're going to pay for what you've done to my girl."

Neil punched him in the gut a couple of times, then each guy took turns working him over as he cried and begged for mercy.

Neil asked him, "How does it feel to beg and cry, and knowing when we're done with you that you are going to be fish food?"

He passed out and got water thrown on his face again until he came back around. He got worked over some more.

Then Neil asked him, "Are you ready to go swimming now?"

Frantically, the guy shook his head no, gasping for air, saying, "I can't, I can't swim!"

"I don't care that you can't swim," Neil said. "Why should I care?"

Bull then walked up, wrapping his arms around the guy, picking him up, as another untied him from the rope. Bull slung him over his shoulder, cement bucket and all, and started heading for the lake. The guy was now in full panic, squirming and yelling.

Got to the edge of the lake. Neil got behind Bull and grabbed the a——hole by his hair and pulled his head up, looking at him in his face.

"Now," Neil said. "You have a choice: swim with the fishes or go away and never come back and forget you ever met my daughter."

Frantically, he replied, "I'll go away, I'll never come back, I swear! Please don't do this, please!"

"I don't know," Neil replied. "I think you're lying to us. What do you guys think?"

Everyone pretty much replied with the same sentiments.

"Say hello to Nemo, a——hole," Neil said.

With that, Bull threw the guy into the water as he was screaming "No!" He sank to the bottom rather quickly with the cement block and log chain, especially as the water was only about three feet deep.

Everyone is laughing hysterically as he stands up in the water, sputtering and freaking out, along with pissing himself.

Neil walks up to the edge of the water and kneels and says, "Okay, this is how this is going to work. You'll be escorted to a bus station and put on a bus with a one-way ticket to California, where you can stay with the rest of the idiots of society. Don't you ever come back here again, and don't ever let us hear about you again, or the next time we'll throw you over there in the deep end. Do you understand?"

"Yes," he answers.

"Yes what?" Neil yells.

"Yes, sir!"

With that, Bull reaches in and drags the guy out of the water.

Neil gives him a hammer and tells him to break himself out of the cement. "We'll be waiting to escort you to the bus station."

The guy was driven to the bus station with nothing but the dirty clothes he had on. The guys waited for the bus to depart, making sure he was on it.

The work was coming along very well. The septic, water, drainage, and wiring were installed. Tunnels were dug out to various access points in the woods, in buildings around the ranch, and coming out on hillsides camouflage openings. Fresh air shafts with level 4 filtration systems. Backup generators and battery banks, with solar panel pods and small turbine wind generators that can be deployed if or when necessary.

Each day, containers were arriving and being prepared to be buried. One at a time they were being lowered, stacked, configured, and welded together for strength. Most of the containers were finished on the inside for the purpose that they were to serve as berthing areas, kitchens, offices, living quarters, restrooms and showers, control centers, and storage rooms. All interconnected. The containers were also bridged to form large garage-parking areas.

It was a wonderfully designed underground compound, and it was deep enough to maintain an average temperature year-round. Just had to maintain the humidity about 40 percent for comfort. Yes, it was all coming together nicely. In another week, the team should be able to start with encasing it all in concrete then burying it.

Boomer and I were looking over the schematics and plans when Aubrey came walking up, greeting us with her beautiful smile and a hug, and said, "I went and scoped out that heroin kitchen that you went to check out a couple of weeks ago. It appears to be pretty heavily guarded. I'd say from the traffic I saw coming and going and supplies going in, it's probably a pretty high-volume kitchen."

"Okay," I replied. "We'll be having a meeting this evening with the guys and discuss when we want to hit them. Please keep an eye on them and notify us of any changes."

"Will do," Aubrey said, as she handed us a rolled-up sheet of paper. "This is the layout of their kitchen and the surrounding area that I could get. Do you want me at the meeting, Rip?"

"Yes, I do," I replied. "Your input is vital to making this a safe success. We'll see you at 1900 hours."

Her little face gleamed with that beautiful smile, as she put her little lethal fist up to bump fists with us, and away she went.

* * *

In the briefing room, everyone was gathered and ready. With the layout diagram on the board, we planned our operation.

According to Aubrey, it appeared they were prepared for us to attack as they had backup stationed a couple of blocks away from the site that could respond at a moment's notice.

Looking at Peyton, I asked, "Do you think your snakes can help us out with this? We don't want their reinforcements to arrive until we are gone."

Grinning from ear to ear, Peyton said, "Oh, I'm sure we can make them reconsider their actions. I think the cobras would be perfect. I'll put them in their cars."

"Well, you are the snake charmer," I replied. "We'll let you handle that. You and Aubrey can work out the details and cover each other's six." I turned to the rest of the team. "Okay, ladies and gentlemen, any more questions? Unless something changes, we'll hit them tomorrow night. Meet here at midnight. You guys have done incredible work on the compound the past month, and we are way ahead of schedule. Go out and enjoy yourselves, and rest up for this op. After we complete this I want you all to take a couple of days off and relax. I'll be down at the bar. Rose is working tonight, so drinks are on me."

I walked into the bar. It was a busy night, and Rose had her hands full keeping up with customers. She is a hard worker and very efficient. I certainly couldn't do her job just because I don't have the patience with people, let alone obnoxious drunks. But she smiles and presses on yet doesn't hesitate to put them in their place when they are out of line.

She smiled at me as she approached with my drink in hand, touched my hand, and gave me a peck on the lips.

I said, "The team is coming down in a little bit. Put their drinks on my tab tonight."

"What's going on?" she asked.

"We have a job tomorrow night, so they're coming out and relaxing until then," I replied.

"Do you need me to help, babe?" she asked.

"No, we've got it handled, unless of course you want to work with Peyton and Aubrey. Maybe drive them to their drop-off."

"Sure, I can do that." She smiled.

I began chuckling. "You'll have a full car."

She looked at me questioningly.

"You will have Aubrey and Peyton and about four or five king cobras," I said.

All of a sudden, that gorgeous smile disappeared, and she raised her voice in protest. "Oh, hell no, no, no, no! Isn't a chance in holy hell!" Her whole body reacted to imaginary slithery things touching her body.

So being the ass that I am, I ran my finger up the back of her bare arm and made hissing noises when she was not looking, and she quickly slapped my hand away, still creeped out. I was laughing uncontrollably as the team began filtering in.

Rose yelled at Peyton as she walked in, "Honey, can you give me a hand here?"

Peyton jumped behind the bar and helped Rose with everything. I watched the team interact, and I felt happy for the first time in a long time.

The following night, we suited up, checking our equipment and weapons with silencers. We were putting two snipers in place before our arrival. The ladies had the cobras in the car and were ready to head out as we climbed into the vehicles.

We entered the quiet neighborhood and parked on opposite sides of the block to approach on foot as to surround the house. Hiding in the shadows, I radioed Peyton to check that everything was ready.

Peyton said, "Yes, we're ready, and these guys have unexpected guests waiting for them in the cars when they get in."

Chuckled to my self, thinking, *I don't think I'd want to piss her off.*

"Okay, don't hesitate to take them out and you two be careful," I said.

Then I radioed S1 and S2. "You two ready up there? Take them out on my command. Team 2, are you ready?"

"S1 ready, S2 ready, team 2 standing by on command."

Looked back at my team and got a thumbs-up.

"Okay, S1, S2, take out targets," I said.

S1 replied, "Two targets down, clear."

S2 replied, "Three targets down, clear."

"Team 2, move," I said.

I led my team to the front door. Breaching the door, we entered, dropping targets as we advanced. One room at a time, we cleared them. The kitchen was in the basement. We dropped a flash-bang through the basement door and stepped back as it went off. We headed down.

Gunfire erupted, and multiple targets fired wildly as they were disoriented. Dropping into prone positions and from behind cover, we fired back with pinpoint accuracy, dropping multiple targets. The kitchen workers had their hands up in the air in surrender. Ordered them to get on the floor facedown with their hands locked behind their heads. The team quickly zip-tied their wrists and ankles. Team

2 was going from room to room, taking cash stashes hidden in walls, heat ducts, floorboards, and false ceilings.

Once everyone was secured, team 1 also did the same in the basement. There were stacks of heroin bags and products, along with stacks of cash in what appeared to be a counting room. This was a huge haul, just what we found, not counting what team 2 found on the upper levels. The entire operation took less than five minutes, and we were leaving the building. Not a neighbor in sight.

Checked in with Peyton.

She replied, "We're good here. Seven targets down, two of them incapacitated and will be dead soon. Cobras are happy. We'll meet you back at the base."

Upon returning to base, we cleaned the weapons and stowed them. Boomer and I counted the cash and were shocked at the amount of money that was confiscated. It didn't seem right; we expected a large amount but not $17 million. There was something else here.

"What do you think, Boomer?"

"I don't know, Rip," he replied. "I would think it would have been better protected than it was, unless the offsight goons that the girls took out were their ace, not suspecting we would be on to them."

"Well, no one ever said these idiots had much sense," I said. "Okay, well, we'll split up half into the war fund and then split the other half between everyone. The war fund was getting low with the expenses of the compound. That'll be a big help. By the way, we need to get a couple more guys added to our ranks. We can't leave the compound unprotected, and we'll need more guys for bigger operations."

Boomer nodded his head in agreement. "I'll get to work on that. I have a couple in mind."

Went out into the conference room with the team, getting everyone's attention. "If you guys want to line up," I announced. "It's payday!"

I stepped outside while they were getting paid, and I heard "Hey there, handsome, you got a light?"

Turned and looked to see this perfect figure of a woman slowly walking toward me out of the darkness, and of course it was Rose. I looked in awe as she approached me with that smile. Every time was like the very first time I saw her.

My pulse quickened, and I felt giddy. Okay, okay, maybe a small touch of drool in the corner of my mouth. I'm a guy, what do you expect? I reached out and embraced her and held her tight, feeling her heartbeat and the warmth of her breath on my neck. Feeling complete as we just stood there soaking in our oneness.

CHAPTER 7

It was a beautiful morning, and the team was at work on the compound, getting it prepared for the cement to be brought in. Last-minute welding and touch-ups were being done as I strolled through, scoping out the awesome compound that we had to work out of. I was impressed by the work these guys had done in a short time.

I came across Cowboy and Neil working on some electronics in the control room.

"Neil, how's your daughter doing?" I asked.

Neil, smiling, said, "She's doing well. She's home and healing. She asked what happen to Scott. I just told her he moved to California. He won't be back."

"What did she say to that?" I asked.

"She was relieved, she didn't have to worry anymore," he replied.

"Well, you tell her for now on that her uncles are going to vent her boyfriends before she dates them," I said, smiling.

"Already told her." Neil laughed.

Turning to Cowboy, I asked, "So when are we going to start bringing in the concrete?"

"We are filling in large areas with dirt and putting up forms," Cowboy said. "I'd guess that the day after tomorrow we'll be ready to pour. We have just a few things to do on the outside. Almost everything else is on the inside that we can do anytime, but I'd say by the end of the week, we will be fully functional."

"That's great news," I replied. "Great work, buddy." I patted him on the back as I headed out the door.

Getting back topside, I saw Boomer was waiting for me. "Hey, Rip, remember the FBI agent I told you about from the kids that we rescued last month?"

"Yeah, Special Agent Blye, wasn't it?" I asked.

"Yes, that would be him. Well, I just got off the phone with him. Rip, he wants to meet up with us as soon as possible."

"He called you?" I asked.

"Yes, he called me," Boomer replied. "I don't know how he knew me or where to find me, but Rip, he asked to meet with you as well—by name."

"Sh——t, this can't be good," I replied. "Call him back. Set up a meeting someplace we can post a few of our guys to cover us. Either we have an inside mole, or we're being followed."

"I have to agree with you, Rip," Boomer replied. "I can't believe we have a mole, but I'll set up a meeting."

The next day, we headed to a park where we were to meet with Special Agent Blye. We already had a dozen of our people in place, watching for any sort of a trap by the Feds. And to assist us in escaping should anything go south.

Boomer and I pulled into the park and looked around as we were getting out of the Jeep. We could see joggers and guys playing basketball, guys playing Frisbee, guys sitting on the park benches talking, all looking very normal, blending in with the civilians. We headed toward the fountain, where we agreed to meet.

"S1, S2, do you see anything yet?" I asked.

"Negative," they both replied.

"Keep your eyes open, and give us a heads-up when you see them or anything out of place."

We didn't have to wait long when S2 said, "Black SUV approaching from the north unit 1."

We spotted them coming into the park and pulling into the parking space. Four men dressed in suits got out and came walking our way, looking around as they got nearer. Boomer recognized Agent Blye leading the group.

Blye reached his hand out and introduced himself to me. He shook Boomer's hand, smiling, and said, "It's good to see you again in a little-less-tense situation." Looking back at me, Agent Blye said, "First I want to thank you for the work you and your team are doing. As unethical that it is illegal, you guys are cleaning up the riffraff. Your rescue of those children was commendable, and because of that operation, I was promoted from special agent to special agent in charge of the Missing and Exploited Children Unit. The reason I wanted to meet with you, we wanted to know if you possibly would be willing to work with us."

Looking at Boomer and back at the agent, I asked, "So you're not here to take us in?"

"No," he answered. "I'm here to offer you a contract basically to be our unofficial long arm. We are bound by our code of conduct and ethics and procedures. You, however, are not. We are aware of the base compound that you've built, and we certainly see the determination that you and your team have, and it's very commendable. Listen, we will supply you with information and funds, whatever you need. The upper crust of the FBI, like the government, is compromised and cannot be trusted. This is strictly between us. Are you interested, Rip?"

"How do we know that we can trust you?" I replied.

"I'm going to give you a gift, a piece of the puzzle that you've been working on. The hit on your family wasn't orchestrated by the WarDogs. They just carried it out, but it's not completely cut and dry as that. There is a drug cartel that's involved in this, but it was an insider that gave you up to them and directed the hit. So, are you interested, Rip?"

"Give us a minute, please." I pulled Boomer off to the side. "What do you think, Boomer?"

"Man, I don't know," Boomer replied. "If he's being straight with us, it would be great, but how do we know it's not a setup?"

"Boomer, he knows our operation, and if he wanted us busted, I believe he'd have already done it. I say we go with it carefully. Besides, what are the options? If we say no, he could pop us for what they already know we've done. What do we have to lose at this point?"

"Agreed," Boomer replied. "Let's see what he has to say."

I turned back to Agent Blye. "Okay, we can try this. What are you offering us?"

Agent Blye smiled and said, "Great. First off, the piece of the puzzle, I promised you. Sergeant Keifer from the Special Victims Unit is the piece you are missing. He gave you and your family up to the cartel."

Instant rage surged through my body. That little snake. I remembered his arrogant, pompous, holier-than-though attitude. We knew it was one of four officers.

I should have known it was him, I thought. *I'll take care of him.*

Looking at the agent, I said, "Thank you for that. Do you have a mole in my team, or how did you get this information on us and know that I was alive?"

"Honestly, we suspected it when you hit the child-smuggling operation, but we weren't sure, so we have been watching the bar where Rose works, suspecting you couldn't resist going in. So we bugged the place and heard you coming out to Rose. Whoever your surgeon is did a great job on you. Certainly an improvement from your official military photos." He laughed.

"What we'll also do, we'll put you and your team on an unofficial payroll," Blye continued. "I will be your liaison. Your only contact, these men and I, will work with you along the way. Now a lot of these operations will be across the country, so you will need mobile command posts and support vehicles. I don't know what weaponry you have or need, but you come to me when you figure it out. Anything you confiscate in an operation is yours except for the drugs. We'll dispose of it, and we'll cover you as much as possible."

"We will have to discuss this with the team, but I'm sure they'll agree to it," I replied.

"Great," Special Agent Blye said. "Also keep in mind though, plausible deniability. Should you or any of your team be captured by our or another department, we don't know you. With that said, we have a field agent embedded in a smuggling ring of kids in Cleveland. I do believe that you will want to stop their shipment that we suspect will happen within the next week. I will keep you posted of any updates, and I'll get you the layout of where they are being kept—of course, pending that your team agrees to this venture."

I reached out and shook Special Agent Blye's hand, and we shook the other agents' hands as well.

"We'll be in touch," Special Agent Blye said.

They turned and walked away, waving in the general direction of our support team around us.

As they drove off, I informed the support team to wrap it up and meet back at the base.

* * *

Upon returning to the base, we called for the rest of the team working on the compound to join us in the conference room. Rose, Peyton, and Aubrey were working on finishing touches inside the living areas of the compound, and they also came and joined us.

Once everyone was present and seated, Boomer and I relayed what Special Agent Blye had told us, and I left it to the team. "You guys discuss this among yourselves."

Meantime, I pulled Rose off to the side and said, "So if you want, you are officially part of this team, and you'll be paid a healthy salary. You do not have to bust your little ass anymore dealing with loudmouth, obnoxious drunks. You can keep the job as a cover. Just a thought."

Rose replied, "The bar is for sale, so I may not have a job depending on who buys it."

"Well, do you want to buy it?" I asked.

Rose, now deep in thought. "I wouldn't mind buying it, but my credit sucks, and I sure don't have $250K to buy it with."

"Well, you do need something to use as a cover as far as your income and so forth. People will want to know where you get your money from. Certainly can't say 'I'm a hit woman for the FBI.'" I laughed.

Chuckling, Rose agreed. "This is true, but how?"

I replied, "Your credit score is great with me. I'll give you the money to buy it and make any upgrades and improvements that you want to make."

"On one condition," Rose replied. "You let me pay you back with interest, or no." She looked at me sternly in the eye.

"You do know that you're a brat and that I am incapable of saying no to you," I replied, laughing.

She reached up with both hands behind my neck, looking into my eyes, and pulled me to her, kissing my face, saying, "Thank you."

Suddenly, we heard a roomful clearing their throats and laughing.

"Come on, you two," Peyton said. "You're killing my eyes."

I chuckled. "Okay, okay, so what's the verdict?"

"We're in, it's unanimous. Let's go kick some asses," came from the back of the room.

Everyone froze and turned to look at Bull.

"Holy sh———t," I said. "You *do* speak!"

"I've got a voice in this too, don't I?" He grinned his growling grin.

"Yes, my giant friend, you most certainly do," I replied. "You most certainly do."

* * *

Watched the concrete being poured in and around the compound sides, one truck after another all being driven and operated by our people for security purposes.

Boomer approached with a folder. "Here's the information from SA Blye. Looks like this one is going to be an all-hands operation, Rip." He lays the information out on the table.

Looking at the layout, I could see it was a fairly large area, and the kids were at the center. "We are going to have a large distance to cover to get to the kids in a normal raid, which's going to put them at high risk before we're going to be able to reach them. The moment they spot us, they'll move in on the kids.

"We're going to need to air-drop a team directly on top of this building and enter here, through the top and rappel from the roof into the windows on all four sides simultaneously, and set security for these kids until the rest of us clean up the garbage. Just before the drop, snipers will have to take out the lookouts. Have Hawk find us a bird so we can drop eight men on that roof."

"Are we going to extract these children out or leave the locals to take care of them again?" asked Boomer.

"No, we'll leave it to locals to take care of them, and we'll just provide cover until they arrive," I replied. "We'll commandeer a couple of city dump trucks to use as a battering ram and draw fire as our guys take out the gunmen as they come out. Have Neil check into the bankroll for these kids."

"Already did that, Rip, it's a huge dollar amount," Boomer replied. "We're talking, like, around fifty million."

Shaking my head in disgust, I said, "Okay, let's get the guys together this evening and lay it out to them. Get their input, and we'll determine when we are going to strike."

* * *

That evening, we were all gathered, and the plan was laid out. Hawk was going to get us a plane and drop team 1 about five miles out, and they would glide in undetected. Teams 2 and 3 would come in from the opposite sides using dump trucks as battering rams. No drivers, just a stick on the gas pedals and the steering tied off, causing maximum confusion and division in their compound as we plucked them off in a shooting gallery.

"Snipers, primary mission after the initial taking out their lookouts, and team 1 is on target," I said. "Eliminate all gunmen approaching the building the kids are in while meantime taking out any ground targets as fast as possible. Otherwise, wrap it up fast! There will be an FBI agent in the area most likely. We'll work out the details with them to not accidentally take him out.

"Now, I want to discuss something with you guys to see how you feel about it. Up until now, we've taken the money from these operations involving the kids. We've paid ourselves well, and we've built this compound using said money from it and the drug raids. Now that we are going to be paid well for what we do, I propose that all the money we confiscate from child trafficking that we set up a fund for those victims. College scholarships, counseling, treatments, and so on. Anything we can do to help them heal from the atrocities that they've endured."

Looked at the faces across the room. Everyone was nodding their heads in agreement. Looking at our three beautiful ladies, I saw tears welling up in Aubrey's blue eyes.

"Aubrey, would you like to spearhead this program?" I asked.

Aubrey smiled and said, "I'd be honored to."

Rose and Peyton both in agreement also said they want to help with this.

"Neil, would you please set up an account specifically for this and handle anything else these ladies need in that area?" I asked. "So when you transfer the money from the traffickers it goes into a safe account that can't be traced back to their origins."

"You got it, Rip," replied Neil.

"Great," I replied. "Enjoy your night off. Meet up tomorrow back here at 2200 hours to prep. Unless SA Blye says different, the op will begin at 0200. Team 1 reports to the airfield of Hawk's choice by 0030. I'll be joining team 1 for this op. See you guys tomorrow evening."

Rose approached me as the team was socializing, deciding who was buying the first round. We took hands and walked outside into the moonlight. It was a chilly night. As I felt Rose shudder, I slipped my jacket off and wrapped it around her shoulders. I leaned against the rail as she leaned into me, and I held her tight, trying to keep her warm. Her head tucket into me, and I placed a warm kiss on her forehead.

"For your information," I said, "I deposited $300K into an account for the bar and renovations. It's not in your name, but you and I are the only ones with access to it. You can draw from it to make payments monthly, down payment, renovations—whatever you need it for."

"Thank you, babe," Rose replied. "I'll be talking to the owner in the morning to get this started. I can't believe how much life has changed since you came back."

"I know," I replied. "I'm sorry."

She quickly nudged me in the gut. "You better not be sorry," she said. "I couldn't be much happier."

I held her close with all my heart.

The next morning, the crew was applying a sealant on the concrete dome of the compound before burying it in a couple of days. A couple of other guys were out in the surrounding areas, testing and tweaking sensors and thermal or night vision cameras in conjunction with the control center.

Boomer and I were out grooming the horses.

I asked, "Anything from SA Blye?"

"Yes," Boomer replied. "He contacted the agent and informed him that we'll be hitting tonight. That agent will be wearing an infrared band around his right arm just above his elbow so we'll be able to spot him with the night vision. He'll also try to be in the building with the kids so he can assist from the inside."

"That's great," I replied. "When we meet at 2200, I'll make sure everyone is up to date."

CHAPTER 8

"So what do you think, Boomer?" I asked. "Things are coming together pretty well, don't you think?"

Boomer replied, "We're moving into a new phase here. Expanding into bigger things, I believe. Soon as we fill in the hole above the compound, we'll start laying the form down for concrete flooring for the machine shed right above the cave."

"The cave?" I asked.

"Yes. Instead of the compound, I'm calling it the cave."

"Okay, the cave it is," I said. "When this op is complete, we'll have to sit down and start making out a list and strategy of what we need to become more mobile."

"Yes, Boomer replied. "I have some ideas."

"I figured that you would," I replied. "As do I. We'll compare notes and see what we've got."

We entered the conference room close to 2200, and the guys were already preparing and testing communication on the primary com system and backup. Everyone was updated on the agent in play as being friendly on the inside and his infrared marker band.

"Last word before we head out to get on station," I said. "Protect those children, and protect that agent and each other. Don't get dead. Neil, how's your end coming?"

Money has already been transferred into this account the FBI gave us the numbers to," Neil answered. "So the transfer should begin anytime."

"Okay," I replied. "When we begin the raid, you transfer the money as I instructed into a safe account. Okay, team 1, go ahead and head to the airport with Hawk. Snipers 1 and 2, take your positions upon your arrival. Do we have the dump trucks lined up?"

"Yes, sir," replied Cowboy. "They are staged about a block away from our target."

"Outstanding," I said, as I was looking around. "Aubrey, my little secret weapon, are you ready?"

"Yes, I am," she replied.

"I want you to be on standby close to the target. Primarily to move in after we secure the facility and assist in protecting the kids and to help soothe them once the sh——t hits the fan, but don't hesitate to take out any gunmen that come into view. If there are no questions, let's go."

The team headed out the door. Rose stood by the doorway. I stopped and hugged her tight.

She whispered, looking into my eyes, "Please be careful. I'll be waiting here for you when you get back."

I smiled and kissed her perfect lips. We exchanged our heartfelt I love yous, and I went out the door to catch up with team 1.

We arrived at the airport, and Hawk already had the plane preflight and prepared to take off. We made last-minute adjustments and, tightening up straps, made sure our infrared markers were working. We climbed into the plane and sat along the sides as Hawk began to accelerate. The plane shuddered and shook like an old milk crate as it gained speed. We lifted off the ground, and it smoothed out, and we began to climb.

We were listening on the coms to teams 2 and 3 on the ground, taking positions and waiting for our entrance into the theater. The timing had to be right. Our ears were popping as we gained altitude, and then Hawk looked back at us.

"Okay, gentlemen," Hawk said. "We're approaching the drop point. Stand by."

We all stood and moved toward the door. As we opened the door, the wind ripped through the cabin.

"S1 and S2, how does it look down there on target?" I asked.

"S1, good."

"S2, good."

"Okay, hold fire until we're one minute from touchdown." Then Hawk yelled, "Go!"

One behind the other, we stepped out the door into the night, free-falling toward the theater coordinates. Gliding together in a *V* formation, we spread our winged suits and steadied our descent. Nearing time to pull the rip cords. We separated a short distance to allow room for the chutes to open.

One at a time, we deployed the black chutes without incidents. Two minutes to touchdown, I announced, "Snipers standby."

"S1, roger."

"S2, roger."

"Team 2 standing by."

"Team 3 standing by."

I could see the set infrared markers. "Okay, guys. One minute."

"S1, target down."

"S2, target down."

"Aubrey, two targets down," I said.

From our view, we could see the dump trucks from both teams crashing through the barricades with sparks flying. Gunmen running out of the buildings, headed toward the trucks firing, desperately trying to stop the unmanned trucks just as we touched down unopposed on top of the building.

S1 and S2 still fired at targets on the ground as teams 2 and 3 entered the open barricades, cutting down everyone who moved. We were quickly gathering the chutes and taking protective cover and preparing to rappel into the windows below, anchoring our ropes and getting into position on all four sides of the building.

"Okay, team 1, GO!" I yelled.

Everyone kicked out and swung in through windows, firing at gunmen being caught by surprise. I spotted the infrared marker band on one gunman and acknowledged him. He returned acknowledgment and turned the fire on the other gunmen. Once the path was cleared, he waved us to follow him.

Occasionally there were dropping gunmen here and there who popped in on us. The agent arrived at a door that was barred.

He said, "They're down here."

"Okay," I said. "Form a perimeter until this theater becomes inactive, as there is still gunfire around outside. Aubrey, we need you in here now."

One of the guys wrapped a zip cord around the bars and took cover and yelled "Fire in the hole!" as he lit the end of the cord. Quickly, the cord flared up and disintegrated the bars holding the door closed.

Aubrey entered the room and headed for the door as the agent opened it and headed in. We stayed in place until one by one the teams reported clear.

"S1 and S2, clear."

"Okay, gentlemen, let us get out of here," I said. "Aubrey, you and the agent have this. We've got to go."

We started exiting procedures, as Aubrey stuck her head around the corner, calling for me in a different tone. "Rip, you need to come in here."

I waved for the others to go outside and stand by. I approached the door. Aubrey was looking at me with tears.

I stopped. "What is it?" I asked.

"I don't know what to say, but you have to see for yourself."

I entered the room, and it was full of young girls of all ages, some dressed as prostitutes, others naked, some dressed in rags. My heart sank and was broken as I looked at every face one at a time. They were crying and scared to death, as Aubrey and the agent worked at trying to calm them and assure them that they were safe now.

Then I froze. My heart stopped, and the tears poured down my face. It was my Emily! Oh my god! I'm positive it was Emily! Could my eyes be failing me? It has been a while, and she had grown, plus they had her dressed up with makeup. But she was dead, wasn't she?

I wanted to run to her and hold her tight, but I wasn't trusting myself. Plus she was already traumatized, and I didn't look like her father, and I didn't want to scare her more, especially if I was wrong.

I was trembling as I turned to Aubrey. "Go ask her name."

Aubrey turned to me and said, "I've seen the pictures of your kids. I think it's her, but I'll ask."

Aubrey walked slowly to the girl and was talking to her, but I couldn't hear. The girl answered her, and Aubrey turned to me, and then she smiled.

OH MY GOD, I thought to myself. *Cindy. Where is Cindy?*

Slowly I approached Emily and got on my knees in front of her, looking up at her. "Emily Johnson?"

Looking back at me in my eyes. She stopped crying and was calm.

"Baby, I know you don't recognize me because I changed my looks. Honey, I'm your dad."

Her eyes flew open wide, and she said, "I knew it!" Then she passed out.

I looked at Aubrey and the agent as I caught her in my arms. "I'm taking her with us. Aubrey, look for Cindy." I yelled on the com, "I'm coming out! Plus one!"

I flung Emily over my shoulder and ran out the door. My mind was racing. How could this be? She was dead. What in the actual f——ck was going on?

I was met outside by team 1, as they assisted in getting us out of there. We could hear the sirens approaching as we disappeared into the night.

The whole drive back, I held my baby close as my team looked at us. I kept checking in with Aubrey if she had found Cindy. "If you find her, you do whatever you have to do to get her out of there."

Aubrey replied, "I promise you, Rip, I will."

We arrived back at the ranch, and I got out of the Hummer, still holding Emily. I began yelling for Rose, finding it hard to even speak. The other guys yelled for Rose.

The door flew open, and out ran Rose with fear in her eyes, but she was relieved when she saw me walking. She got to me with a questioning look on her face as I broke and collapsed, crying. "It's Emily, Rose, it's Emily!"

Rose's eyes flew open wide, looking at the girl as she dropped to the ground with us, holding us both. The team stood around us, caught up in our emotions. I tried to gather my strength to stand and carry her in and lay her down, but I was emotionally and physically drained.

Suddenly, I became aware of Bull standing directly in front of us. He knelt and looked into my eyes. "I've got you, brother."

He reached down and took Emily in his arms and headed for the front door. Rose helped me get up on shaking legs looking at me.

"How?" she asked.

"I don't know," I replied. "But I'm going to get answers."

We got a washcloth and washed up Emily's little face as she lay sleeping. I sat on one side, Rose on the other, both of us holding her hands. I explained to Rose how Aubrey recognized Emily from pictures and called me in, and she was trying to find Cindy.

I felt her fingers move and heard a slight groan as I looked at her, and her eyes slowly opened.

"Hello, sleepyhead," I said.

"Daddy?" Emily asked. "Is that you?"

Rose gently squeezed her hand and said, "Hello, sweetheart."

Emily turned her head toward Rose.

Rose reached in and held her close and kissed her face. "Yes, baby, that is your daddy, and you're safe now."

Emily looked back at me and said, "I could see it in your eyes that it was you, Daddy." She began crying, reaching out for me to hold her.

I held her close, assuring her it would be all right. Then she pulled back and looked at me. "Daddy, Cindy! They still have Cindy!"

I looked at Rose and back at Emily. "Where, honey? Where is Cindy?"

"I don't know, but they separated us a week ago. They took her and a bunch of other young girls her age, and I hadn't seen her since."

"How many others, Emily?" I asked.

"I don't know, maybe a hundred," she replied.

"Okay, honey. Okay, I'll find her." I looked at Rose. "Can you stay with her, babe? I want to see if I can get some information from SA Blye."

"You couldn't tear me away," she replied.

I came out of the room, and several of the team were sitting and waiting to see how Emily was doing.

"Boomer," I said, "Cindy is still alive too. Emily said they separated them just a week ago. Get hold of SA Blye and see what he or that other agent knows. Also, this needs to be kept quiet between us and the FBI. If my babies are alive, what about Crystal? And who the hell was in that fire? Now we have three bodies. What the hell is going on, and why? And who the hell was this coroner that signed off that said those bodies were my family and me? I'm going to talk with him myself and Sergeant Keifer."

Looked back toward the room and then at Boomer. "I've been avoiding asking her questions and upsetting her more, but we need answers."

I turned and went back into the room. Rose was sitting on the bed, holding Emily's hand.

"Hey, sweetheart."

They both looked up.

"I hate to ask you this, but it may be particularly important to save your sister. What do you remember about the night they took you from home? Take your time."

Emily looked up at me with tears in her eyes. "Cindy and I were in bed. I was sleeping and woke up to a loud crash and yelling. I jumped toward the door because at first I thought Mom fell and got hurt, but before I could get the door open, my door flew open, and this man grabbed me and slapped me hard and was dragging me out of my room. Someone had Cindy too. Then I heard mom screaming, and I heard a shot, and the guy that had me fell. Then another shot, and the one that had Cindy fell."

She looked at me and said, "Then the policeman came in and took us out to his car and went back in to talk to Mom."

"Was there anyone else there, baby?" I asked.

"I was in the car, and I did see someone else walk in the front door."

"What was your mom doing when you kids went out to the car?" I asked.

"She was talking to your friend," Emily replied.

"My friend?" I asked.

"Yes, the policeman. I remembered him being at the house before with you."

Thought to myself, *It had to be Keifer, that son of a b——tch!*

Emily and Rose were now crying, Rose holding Emily. Fighting back the tears and the rage building in myself, I asked, "What did you hear or see then?"

"I heard another two shots, and the policeman came walking out fast and got in the car. I asked where my mom was, and Cindy was crying, saying, 'I want my mommy.' He said she would be down later to get us, and she was talking to a friend. But, Daddy, when I looked back as we got down the block, I saw fire coming out the front door."

"Do you remember where you went from there?" I asked.

"We went to some house, and a lady and a man came and got us from the car and told us they'd take care of us until Mom came to get us, and we never saw him again until last week, when they came and got those kids and Cindy." Emily was now crying and apologizing. "I'm sorry, Daddy. I tried to take care of Cindy and protect her."

"You have nothing to apologize for, baby. Mone of this is your fault, you understand me? None of it." I took her in my arms and held her little shaking body as she cried uncontrollably.

Rose was so overwhelmed by the pain and grief from us she cried out loud in her pain, saying Cindy's name and trying to hold us both, trying to comfort us.

Later, I came out to find Boomer waiting for me. He had sent the rest of the team on their way but to be on standby, pending what we find out about this other group of kids. I filled Boomer in on what Emily could recall.

"So what do you think, Boomer?" I asked.

"I think we need to chat with Keifer," Boomer said. "He knows you're alive. Whoever that was that walked in the front door most likely was the other body. The coroner has to be in on this cover-up. The two that grabbed the kids from their rooms must have been the bodies I saw carried out."

"Agreed," I replied. "Crystal killed them protecting the girls, and either Keifer or this mystery man killed her and set the fire to cover it up. Did you get ahold of SA Blye?"

"Yes, he will meet with us this afternoon at 1400, at the fifties diner downtown," Boomer replied.

"Okay," I said. "Meantime, have Aubrey track down Keifer. After I talk to Blye, I'm going to talk to Keifer."

I returned to the room to find Emily had cried herself to sleep and Rose lying beside her with her arm around her. I slowly got in bed on the other side of Emily and put my arm over her, peering across at Rose.

She mouthed, "Are you okay?"

"I will be when I find Cindy," I replied. "Thank you."

I reached up, gently touching Rose's face as she closed her eyes, and we both drifted off to sleep.

CHAPTER 9

The next morning, I woke up with my two angels still sleeping. Rose was holding Emily closely. I slowly got out of bed as to not disturb them.

As I left the room, I was met by Boomer. He reached out, putting a hand on my shoulder.

"How are you doing, buddy?" he asked.

"I'm okay," I replied. "This is unbelievable. Is it even real? Is my baby lying in there alive, Boomer? It doesn't seem real like I'm going to wake up. What did you find out? Did you talk to SA Blye?"

Boomer, looking down, replied, "Yes, I talked to him, Rip. He said that there was a group of kids a week prior shipped off to that island."

Looking at Boomer, I replied, "So what are we saying? Does he think Cindy was sent there?"

Nodding his head, Boomer replied, "We believe so. The timing is spot-on, and his sources are pretty sure, although they don't recall her specifically. There were at least 130 kids in that shipment."

Shaking my head, I looked at Boomer and said, "Let's meet up with SA Blye. Time to see how far they are willing to go to support us when we raid that island."

We met with Special Agent Blye at the diner, sitting in a corner booth. It was a pretty slow day, so we had privacy.

Talking to Special Agent Blye, I asked, "So can you get me a layout of this island? We need the island layout and blueprints of any building that we'll be dealing with. Also, we only have twenty-five soldiers to hit them with. I believe we are more than capable of doing the job, but we will want to observe their movements. It's going to be difficult to approach the island undetected. What can you help us with?"

He rubbed his chin, deep in thought, then replied, "Okay, I can get you the layout and the blueprints. Let me make a call really quick. I think I can get you some support. I'll be right back."

He excused himself and stepped outside.

Boomer turned to me and said, "Are you set on this, Rip? Do you think the team is ready for this?"

"Let's see what Blye has to offer and see the layout, then we'll ask the team," I said.

Special Agent Blye came back in and sat down. "Okay," he said. "When you return to your base, you will have the layout of the island and the compound. As we speak, a satellite is being maneuvered into position to get the latest view. Also, I have a drug hit team from the Reagan war-on-drugs era. They are a very successful mercenary team. They have plenty of firepower and assets, especially out at sea.

"Their specialty is intercepting drug smugglers at sea. They have an ocean freighter that they confiscated from smugglers that they use as a base. They will be at your disposal if you want them to assist. Just give me a heads-up, and I'll make the arrangements."

"Okay," I replied. "Thank you. We will certainly be in contact as soon as possible. Thank you again, SA Blye."

Boomer and I returned to the ranch to find Peyton and Aubrey out at the horse barn with Rose and Emily. I stood at the doorway for a few moments and watched. Emily was slowly grooming a horse on one side, Aubrey on the opposite side of the same horse, conversing with Emily. Rose and Peyton were riding a couple of horses around the arena, talking and laughing.

Emily looked my way and smiled from ear to ear as she dropped her grooming brush and ran at me, diving into my arms. "Daddy!" she said.

I held my baby tight. I was overwhelmed that my baby was home and safe.

The ladies approached us as I looked at each one and settled my eyes on Rose.

She asked, "So did you find out anything about Cindy?"

Emily looked up at me as I replied. "We think we know where she is. We are gathering information. We'll be looking over the information that SA Blye is sending us, and then we'll have a meeting with the team. One way or the other, I'm going to get my daughter back, whatever it takes."

After reviewing the information, we met with the team. I looked across the room at my team. Anxiously they waited to hear what we had. We displayed the satellite views and the blueprints for all to see, and we discussed the details of doorways, windows, and building placements.

I filled them in on the mercenary team that was willing to assist us and of their assets we could use to get close.

"We don't know what building that the kids are kept, or how many," I said. "We do know that there were 130 kids shipped over there, but we don't know how many were already there. So, giving what we do know so far, what do you guys think?"

Cowboy looked back at the rest of the team then back up front at us. "Is that even a question? My question is, when the hell do we leave? I don't know about the rest of these guys, but I'm ready for a tropical island vacation."

Neil spoke up. "Hell, yes. I love those coconut drinks with umbrellas and fruit."

Cowboy, laughing, said, "That figures. You would like the fruit, Neil." He reached over and ruffled his hair.

Everyone chuckled.

Cowboy looked at me and said, "Let's go get your daughter, Rip. Let's bring her home."

I wanted to deal with the snake before we go to the island, but Cindy was way more important. We had to hit the island hard and fast before some foreign slimeball got ahold of her for their own pleasure in whatever sh——thole country they came from. I was going to take great pleasure in killing Keifer when I got back. A slow and painful death.

The team worked into the night on plans and positions along with times. This mercenary team would be of great help. Special Agent Blye said they were the best in what they do. We had one of the agents who was going to be able to drop a squad from a plane to glide in as in the last mission. The mercenary team had a fully loaded AH-64 Apache attack helicopter on board their ship for air support if necessary. We had UAV's drones for air surveillance and UGV's drones for on-the-ground surveillance.

The compound was at one end of the island, so the teams would approach the island underwater from two sides while the third squad would parachute in on top of the building we suspected to house the children in. Once the two teams reached shore and positioned themselves, team 1 would drop in. Many important dignitaries come to this island, so heavily armed guards were expected. It was settled: this coming Monday night, we were taking this island.

The following days, the teams had drills and practiced the mission repeatedly until they could do it in their sleep. Aubrey and I, along with five others, would be on team 2, along with S2, as Boomer and his team 3 and S1 would beach on the other side of the island. S1 and S2 would find high ground to nest in and take out targets, setting up a crossfire. I would run the UGV to try and locate the children using infrared to pick up heat signatures, and Boomer would run the UAV from his position also with infrared. Tomorrow morning, we would head down to the coast to rendezvous with the mercenaries. I only pray that we would find Cindy safely.

That night, I started a small fire for Rose and Emily and me. We sat together talking and joking, but I could clearly see that Emily was struggling try to be her normal self. I looked at Rose, and she knowingly returned the look, acknowledging that she could see it too. My baby has been through unspeakable hell and has a long road to recovery. I loved them both, but the whole time was thinking about tomorrow's mission when I would hopefully be able to get Cindy home again.

The next morning, before we left, I met with the security team and told them to be on heightened alert while we were gone.

"Utilize the cave, and keep it locked down," I instructed. "Rose and Emily would stay in the compound also."

* * *

We arrived at the coast and met the leader of the mercenaries named Drake. We shook hands and introduced ourselves.

Drake looked at me and said, "Whatever we have is yours to use, Rip. My crew and I will do whatever we can to support your team. I have a couple of Zodiacs standing by over here to take you and your team out to the ship."

Grabbing our gear, we loaded into the rugged high-speed rubber boats and headed out to sea. After about a half hour, we were approaching the ships bow. Drake radioed the ship just as the front of the ship began opening.

Drake looked at me and said, "This is our garage." He chuckled.

We drove right into the bow as we were met by his crew catching the lines being thrown to them and tying off the Zodiacs. We climbed out as hoists now came down and were attached to the Zodiacs and lifted up out of the way into storage.

Looking around, we could see hydrofoil river gunboats also suspended.

Drake, seeing our curiosity, said, "We will deploy those tonight to drop your teams off closer to the island. Then they will stand by in the dark for emergency extraction or assist any way we can."

Nodding my approval, I said, "You have an awesome setup here, Drake."

He replied, "Thank you. You haven't seen anything yet."

He led us to a ladder and headed up, as we followed.

"I'll take you to meet the crew, and then I'll show you around," Drake said.

Along the way, he explained how they confiscated this ship from a drug lord in Columbia and that they used to use it to launch their drug-packed submarines from the bay that we parked in.

"Of course, we made many modifications and improvements." Laughing, he said, "We had Somalia pirates thinking we were a normal ocean freighter. You can imagine their surprise when they tried to hijack us and board us. None of them survived that attack."

He was still chuckling as we entered a conference room where a dozen rough-looking men got up as we entered.

"This is my crew, gentlemen," Drake said.

My team and his crew introduced themselves, shaking hands and bumping fists. Aubrey silently stood by my side, smiling, as each one of the crew took her hand and gently shook her hand, as if they were afraid to break her. Bull stood like a statue and bumped fists but said nothing.

I said, "These two are my most unique members. First, I'll introduce my secret weapon, and probably the deadliest."

The crew were looking at Bull but were shocked when I introduced Aubrey. They still had that deer-caught-in-the-headlights look as I explained her talents.

Drake, a bit surprised, said, "How can anyone so beautifully perfect be so deadly?"

Cowboy spoke up. "Oh, trust me, mate." He held his throat. "That smiling face is just a trick to lower your guard."

There were a couple of chuckles around the room.

"And this is our prettiest." I turned to Bull. "He doesn't speak much, but his charm alone will kill you." I explained who Bull was and his background in Delta Force. "He's basically a one-man killing machine."

Drake said, "Well, we'll leave our people to get acquainted as I show you around, Rip. Follow me."

We left the room, and Aubrey tagged along with us. We headed to the bridge, where he introduced us to an older gentleman.

"This is the captain. He's a civilian. His only job is to get us in and out of anyplace that we need this ship to go. His first mate assists him, and they take turns on long deployments. This man can parallel park this monster. We'll go down one level to the control center for OPS."

We went down a ladder one level, and Drake used a biometric pad to enter his thumbprint for entry. Stepping in the room was like a high-tech dream. Two men were manning the center, looking back and waving acknowledgment as they were introduced.

"These guys are our IT specialists," Drake said. "They intercept communications from known drug runners and kingpins. Decode and decipher what they are doing and where. As you can see, we also have hidden cameras in various hot spots that we know they frequent. This panel here is the fire control center, pointing out the windows at various places on the ship.

"We have missile batteries hidden from view in those shipping containers. Those containers open up and deploy surface-to-air, surface-to-surface, and even surface-to-subsurface missiles, using various guidance systems such as laser, heat-seeking, radar, and sonar. We also have a single rail gun mounted in the bow just above the doors that we came in with the boats. It'll put a VW Beetle-sized one-ton projectile through any ship over twenty-five miles away. It uses a lot of power, but we figured out a way to keep a capacitor fully charged and ready to deploy the first shot in less than a minute. Otherwise, it takes about five minutes to build up enough juice to fire a shot. Then we also have a modified Falcon system for self-defense against basically anything coming at us from the air, land, or sea."

"Totally impressed with your ship, Drake, you don't mess around," I said.

"These drug lords don't mess around either, we have to be prepared for anything," Drake said. "SA Blye tells me your children were taken by these human traffickers and you recovered one of them, and you think there's one on this island?"

"That's what I'm understanding," I replied. "We'll find out tonight."

"What are you going to do with anyone you capture tonight?" Drake asked.

"There won't be any prisoners," I replied. "They don't deserve to live. My only concern is to recover all of these kids no matter what it takes. Everyone other than the kids are collateral damage. If they are there in the compound and not victims, then they're guilty. I don't care if they are dignitaries from foreign governments or America. Celebrities, athletes, if they are here, they are here to molest little kids. Capturing them would do nothing, and our so-called justice system would do nothing to them. In fact, undoubtedly, they too are involved in this. We know for a fact that Jeffery didn't hang himself, and we know Killary and others in our government had to silence him. The scandal is beyond huge and stretches worldwide. It's despicable."

"Well, you have our support, Rip," Drake replied. "Let's go brief my crew, get your people situated, have a good meal, and rest. I'm sure it's been a long day, then let's go get your daughter."

Back in the conference room, the two groups were as one and fellowshipping as if they'd known each other forever. Drake and I got up in front of the group and called for their undivided attention. One of his crew turned on the huge monitor for all to see. The first slide read "OPERATION CINDY." It was a close-up satellite view of the compound.

Drake said, "Okay, gentlemen and lady"—nodding toward Aubrey—"we are currently ten miles away from the target, just over the horizon due west of our current position. We took the liberty of flying drones over the target last night with infrared and then again today just before your arrival, so as you see here, this building appears to be where these kids are kept at night, as you can see the multiple heat signatures concentrated lying horizontally.

"This building here, we believe, is the ballroom, where the kids are being presented and displayed like cattle to the pervs. Also, see here and here are centuries standing guard. This is one of four guard towers around the compound. Also note, there appears to always be one or two guards on the roof of the building where the kids are. If you are going to drop in on them, they'll have to be taken out the same time the lookout towers are, but silently."

I replied, "These guys are masters at multiple silent kills."

Drake said, "We dropped a couple of hot mics from the drone last night to listen in, and from what we can gather, they are planning a party tonight in the ballroom. Gentlemen, you're going to crash that party."

Looking over the layout and the information Drake had gathered for us, I pointed out our insertion points, and we discussed the logistics of getting everyone into position. This would be, by far, the largest OPS our team has ever taken on. Team 1 will be flown by helicopter to a small airfield on shore, where Special Agent Blye had a pilot standing by with a plane fueled up and ready to go. Teams 2 and 3 will be dropped off on opposite sides of the compound about two miles out, and we'd scuba dive into shore. At the appropriate times, we would paint the targets with an infrared laser for the ship's fire-control center to launch missiles in to take out buildings or any said vehicles.

"Aubrey, you're with me," I said. "If Cindy is in there, she's not going to know me, and she's going to be terrified. I want you to get into these kids and try to keep them calm and together until we secure the compound. I'm counting on you. Team 1 will shut down the perimeter of the building. You may have to take out any unknown targets in the building."

Looking at the team, I said, "Thank you, gentlemen, and a special thanks to Drake's crew. We couldn't do this without you, and in the future, if you have something that you could use assistance with, we are only a call away. Don't get dead, gentlemen and lady. Let's go take these kids home to their families."

With that, Drake announced, "Dinner is served in the galley, my friends."

CHAPTER 10

In 2300 hours, we were mustering in the hangar, fitting ourselves with the scuba equipment. Team 1 was headed for the airfield to rendezvous with the agent. Drake's crews were preparing the hydrofoils for battle if necessary and fueling them up. Aubrey was in the corner, preparing for this assault. She had a whole multitude of weapons laid out before her: throwing stars, knives, a blowgun with very wicked-looking broadhead darts, a samurai sword sharp enough to split hair, a collapsible fighting staff, two sets of black nunchucks, and a few other gadgets I had no idea what they were.

"Have you fitted yourself yet with the scuba equipment, Aubrey?" I asked.

Looking up at me, she replied, "Yes, I have. I'm just tucking this stuff away before I put it on." Then looking into my eyes, she said, "Don't worry, Rip, we'll get her back." She came to me and hugged me close. "And Emily is in great hands. Rose loves that girl as if she were her very own."

"I know," I replied, as I looked around at my amazing team of friends. "These guys are amazing. When this is over, we are all going on vacation. Aubrey, what do you think, Hawaii? I'm buying."

Aubrey's little face lights up with her dazzling smile. "Hell, yeah." She laughed. "I'm going to hold you to that bet."

I took her head in my hands and kissed her little forehead. "You got it, girl. Let's go do this."

The hydrofoils were in the water, and the teams were loading up their equipment and getting prepared to deploy. Drake approached me with a concerned look on his face.

"What's wrong, Drake?" I asked.

"We just got confirmation that this compound has an active antiship missile system—an RGM-84, to be exact."

"They have a Harpoon?" I asked. "Are you sure?"

Drake replied, "Yes, and we aren't positive which building is housing it, but we have an idea that it may very well be the building right beside where the kids are being kept."

Deep in thought, I looked at Drake's concerned face. "Are your defense systems on board here enough to take out these Harpoons should they get launched at you?" I asked.

"Yes, we can drop them out of the sky with great accuracy, but should they get launched against the hydrofoils, they won't stand a chance."

"Okay, you don't have any chaff rounds to fire off, do you, to draw the radar of the Harpoons away from their intended targets?"

"Even if I did, I don't have anything to fire them off with."

"Okay, then we need to locate and destroy that launcher," I said. "What does your Apache carry?"

"A 30 mm chain gun, KA-52 80 mm rocket pods, and eight AGM-114 Hellfires," Drake replied.

"Okay, that's the ticket. I'll get the target painted with a laser, you get your pilot to stand by out of sight and be ready to fire when I give the signal. It'll only take one shot. At a cost of $105K per missile, thank God there's only one Harpoon system."

We quickly briefed the teams on the situation and determined we would have to get the kids away from this building ASAP. Team 1 was listening in on the briefing and stated during their descent they would be scoping out the surrounding area for a safe shelter to move the children to. The ground units would have to secure the compound quickly.

"Let's do this," I said.

The bow of the ship opened wide as the hydrofoils fired up their powerful engines and slowly idled out the door, clearing the opening.

The engines went at full power and lifted onto the skies, and we were underway. We went into the night running dark. Guiding by radar and sonar and night vision.

The crackle of the radios confirmed that team 3's boat was splitting off to circle to the other side of the island into position, and team 1 was in the air waiting for orders. Team 3's boat was approaching their position as our captain came to me and said, "I'll be able to get your team within a mile to drop you. Team 3 will also be about the same distance."

"That's great, Captain, thank you," I replied. "That'll give us approximately forty minutes of dive time to reach shore."

"After I drop you, Rip, we'll retreat back about a mile and monitor your radio traffic," said the captain. "We'll cover you any way we can"

"Team 2, man the gunwales," I said.

The team adjusted their masks and stood at the very edge of the boat. Aubrey took position beside me.

I ordered, "Deploy!"

Everyone flipped overboard into the pure darkness of the night water. We began swimming in the direction of our GPS staying dark. Constantly watching our surroundings with night vision as to not run into any surprises along the way, like hungry sharks looking for a midnight snack. We came across a couple of curious dolphins along the way that kept us company for most of the dive, reassuring us that the sharks would probably not even come near us. One dolphin kept pretty close to Aubrey, probably protecting her, with her being the tiniest of the group. She reached out a couple of times even to pet it as it swam by.

We finally reached shore and immediately took cover and hid our scuba equipment in the brush. We donned our night vision and thermal imaging goggles and scanned our surroundings for any potential threats. I got out the UGV drone and activated it. We received confirmation that team 3 had reached shore and were securing their perimeter. Boomer, with team 3, had activated his UAV drone and was launching it into the night as I launched mine. We could see multiple targets that would have to be taken out, including two roving patrols that were approaching our position.

I motioned for Aubrey to take them out. She donned her blow-gun, and she fired one into the neck of the first guard. As the second one turned to his partner, one of Aubrey's stars found its target in his throat, severing his windpipe and the carotid artery.

She turned to me and grinned and whispered to me, "B——tches."

The UGV was approaching the buildings, and I switched it to thermal and scanned the buildings while Boomer's UAV was scanning from the air.

"What do you see, Boomer?" I asked.

"Rip, there's multiple private helicopters on the helipads, and the pilots are standing by at the NE corner," Boomer said. "The berthing barracks we suspect with the children have roughly fifty kids in there along with a half-dozen handlers. The building beside it has six guards that I can see. Must be where the Harpoon system is at. What do you have, Rip?"

"I'm looking at the ballroom, and it's pretty active. Most are in one room ground level, but I'm seeing heat signatures in various rooms in upper levels, what appears to be bedrooms." Shook my head in disgust, knowing what horror was going on in those rooms. I looked at Aubrey, knowing she too knew what was going on.

"Team 1, deploy," I said.

"Team 1 deploying," came the response.

Boomer said, "Team 1, you have seven targets on the roof of the barracks and four on the party house. Can you take them out, or do you want assistance?"

"Team 3, we got this little buddy. We have them in our sights."

I looked up at the night skies and could see the infrared markers on team 1 descending as they fired their whispers of death.

"Team 3, take out the two guard towers over there just as we took out our two towers," I said.

Total silence.

Team 1 landed on deck on the barracks and immediately covered all four sides of the roof, taking out and leaving targets around them. Two of team 1's members began entering the barracks from the roof, killing people along the way.

"Aubrey." I looked at her. "You need to get in there and do your thing."

Aubrey was already halfway across the grounds like a streak of black lightning.

"S1 and S2, are you in position?" I asked.

"S1, yes sir."

"S2, yes, sir, engaging targets."

"S1 and S2, no one leaves in those helicopters," I ordered.

Drake's voice comes across the radio. "Rip, there are four yachts docked at the south end of the island. We have them secured already."

Team 2 approached the party house, taking out targets as quickly and quietly as possible. We were just getting ready to enter the house when team 1 announced they had the barracks secured and Aubrey was with the kids.

"Roger that, team 1," I replied.

Teams 2 and 3 crashed the party. We entered the ballroom, and there were men and women everywhere with children. There were screams and yelling, and of course, everyone was playing victim. We separated the children away from the adults as team 3 began advancing to the upper levels to clear the rest of the house. Team 1 announced that the perimeter was secure and three of the team was heading for the Harpoon launchpad. The rest of the team and Aubrey were relocating the children out of the barracks to a nearby building that was vacant.

Then Aubrey's voice said, "Rip, she's not in here."

"Okay, then she must be over here somewhere," I replied.

I scanned all the faces in sight but not seeing her. *Oh my god, she must be up in one of those rooms.*

The kids were all moved out to the vacant building to join the others whom team 1 had secured, and team 2 advanced to assist team 3 in clearing the building. It was a huge mansion with many rooms, and we entered each room and closets and bathrooms finding kids with adults. Tying up the adults and locking them in closets and sending the kids down the stairs, where a team member waited to guide them to safety. There were actors, politicians, athletes, heads of state from all over the globe.

Finally, one bastard confronted me, claiming we had no jurisdiction there and that they were outside of international waters. The United States had no right to raid his island.

"I have diplomatic immunity," he kept saying with a very smug and condescending voice. "I'll have you fired for this."

I looked at his arrogant face and the fact that he had more chins than a Chinese phone book. I just couldn't help myself as I shoved my M-16 barrel into his mouth, breaking several teeth. I looked around to make sure all the kids were out of the room as I smiled and said, "No, you're fired," as I pulled the trigger.

Reports were coming back from the team members as they cleared the mansion. I headed to where all the children were gathered and looked them all over. Heartbreaking. They were scared and crying and hurt, physically abused, mentally tortured, and an emotional mess. Crying for their parents and each other.

I called for confirmation from everyone. "Is this all of them? Do we have all the children here?"

One by one, it was confirmed. Cindy was not there. I must have been too late. She must have been taken away, somewhere else in the world. Very distraught, my mind racing.

The sound of Boomer's voice. "Rip, you need to see this."

"Where are you?" I replied.

"Up the hall from you," Boomer answered.

I headed up the hall, and I heard Boomer say, "In here."

I walked into this room with monitors all over the wall. "What's all of this?" I asked.

"These are monitors to all the playrooms in this place. Rip, they record every single sexual encounter and keep it. So every person of influence or power or money has a recording of them. They blackmail these people to sway politics, policies, throw games."

Boomer looked around the room. "Rip, this is evil power over control. Let's gather it all up and take it with us."

"Have the rest of the teams sweep this place one more time and make sure we don't miss anyone," I said.

"Already in progress, Rip."

On the radio, I asked, "Team 1, you have that Harpoon secure?"

Team 1 replied, "Yes, Rip, Bull took out the control center himself."

"Great work, guys," I replied. "Let's get the kids down to the docks, and then we're going to level this place."

Aubrey headed everyone toward the docks and began loading them on the yachts. I looked at Aubrey.

"I'm sorry, Rip," I said. "I went through them all, she just isn't here."

"Not your fault," I replied. "What is the final head count?"

"It's 343 kids, Rip. We saved 343 kids that are going to get to go home."

I was happy for them, but I couldn't help but wonder where Cindy was at and how I was going to be able to find her now.

The captains to the yachts were given an offer they couldn't refuse: pilot the boats for us or die. Naturally they couldn't refuse. They were instructed to go to the coordinates where Drake's ship was waiting while a team member watched over them. After all the evidence was loaded onto the last boat and everything was clear, we cast off and radioed Drake.

"Light her up, brother," I said.

The Apache suddenly appeared on the horizon, taking aim at the Harpoon launch pad, and fired a series of Hellfire missiles. They left a trail of fire as they left the Apache out and up then straight down into the launch pad, exploding a thunderous rolling explosion, shooting debris into the sky. Then launched the rocket pods into the buildings, where the pedophiles were screaming for mercy.

Then Drake gave the order to clear the range. The night sky lit up in a blinding flash as he fired off his rail gun at the mansion, and the mansion ceased to exist. Everything shook—the ground, the water, and even the heavens stood still. The hydrofoils escorted the yachts to the ship and stayed on patrol around the area.

Once on board the ship, we met in the conference room. There were a couple of minor injuries to the team, but it all got put on hold while the children were all attended to medically. We were feeding them and trying to comfort them. Aubrey and one of the team members were getting the names of the children and any information we could along with pictures of each of them. Then all this was sent to Special Agent Blye so he could start contacting parents and arrange for transportation for them all.

Drake approached me as I was standing and watching the team talk to these kids and reassure them they would be going home soon. Drake looked around, shaking his head in disgust. "How can those animals do this to these children?"

"I don't know," I replied. "But we are going to do anything we can to stop it. It's a very lucrative business, and it's worldwide. We didn't even dent the surface here."

Boomer walked up to us and said, "We have taken almost a billion dollars in cash from that compound, and I know there was more that we missed. Neil is working on tapping into their offshore accounts. Rip, there's billions and billions."

"Well, we will give some of it to Drake and his crew, and the rest will go into the account to take care of these kids," I replied.

Drake shook his head. "Oh, no, we won't accept a penny. Consider it our contribution."

"You are a class act, brother." I shook Drake's hand.

Then Drake said, "By the way, those yachts are yours, Rip, if you want them. We already have several. I'll have my IT guys process the registrations over to you from the owners. Since they are dead, they won't be needing them. We will keep them at our base as long as you want or until you develop a base of your own."

In disbelief, I thanked Drake again.

The next morning, I was awakened from the sound of helicopters coming on board. I worked my way to the helipad to find Special Agent Blye getting off one of the choppers, then my team and Drake's crew unloading cases of food and supplies.

Special Agent Blye shook our hands and said, "You guys didn't leave a thing alive on that island. Holy sh——t, man!"

"Are you complaining?" I asked.

Laughing, Blye replied, "No, I don't have to do the paperwork or explain anything to anyone how or why these rich and famous pieces of sh——t simply vanished. Since officially this island doesn't even exist, nothing official will be filed. Listen, Rip, I may have some information for you on your daughter. Let's talk."

"I'm listening," I replied.

"I had an informant tell me that there was a police officer that regularly visited that facility you guys hit recently, and he had an interest in a young girl, about six years old. My source told me that they seem to know each other, so I showed my source a picture of Cindy. Rip, he said he thinks that it was her, but he can't swear to it. Now it's just possible that he may have her for himself."

My blood was boiling. "Sergeant Kiefer," I said. "I can almost guarantee it. I'm planning on having a chat with him anyways."

Special Agent Blye replied, "Well, I'll give you a lift back to shore."

Looked at Boomer. "You got this, brother?" I asked.

"I got this, Rip, you go."

Aubrey walked up, looking at me. "I'm going with you," she said.

"No, Aubrey, you're needed here. I've got this," I replied.

Special Agent Blye turned and walked toward the awaiting helicopter.

* * *

The helicopter lifted off the deck and headed west, and a million things were running through my head, but it was all about getting my little girl back and destroying anything and anyone that gets in my way.

As we landed, a Black Tahoe pulled up. Me and Special Agent Blye got in and headed to the airport to head home. I called Rose to inform her on the results of the raid and of my suspicions of the snake, Kiefer.

"How's Emily doing, babe?" I asked.

"She's having nightmares, Rip," Rose replied. "Bad ones. I contacted a very highly recommended therapist, and he will be coming out to talk with us in a couple of days. After what she's told me so far of what she's been through, I may need a therapist too."

Hearing Rose's voice breaking was heart-wrenching because I knew it was bad.

"I love you, Rose. Thank you for being there for her, and me. I'll see you real soon."

CHAPTER 11

When I arrived back at the ranch, Rose and Emily were there to greet me. Hugging and kissing their little faces, I asked Rose if she thought Peyton could stay with Emily tonight.

Looking at Rose, I said, "We have a mission tonight."

"I'm sure she'll be glad to," Rose said. "I'll get someone to cover her shift at the bar tonight. Let me make a couple of calls." She excused herself.

I turned to Emily. "How are you doing, baby girl?"

She looked up at me with those big blue eyes. "I'm okay, Dad. Are we going to find Cindy?" she asked.

"I'm trying, baby, I'm trying."

She grinned back at me and said, "I can't get used to your new face and calling you Dad. I know it's you, but I don't know, it's just weird."

Chuckling, I replied, "I know. Imagine how I feel when I get up in the morning and look into the mirror to shave and wonder who that is looking back at me."

Laughing now, she looked at me and said, "Well, it sure is an improvement, Dad."

I attacked her and wrestled with her a little. "You little sh——t," I said.

Rose came walking back to us and said, "Peyton will be more than glad to. She'll be over here around nine tonight."

"Great," I replied. "Meantime, I am going to take my formally hideous ass in and get a shower and lie down for a nap." I looked over at the giggling Emily.

"Rose told me to say that, Dad. I'd never say something like that."

Looked over at Rose with my eyebrow up. "Really? Rose, are you telling my daughter I was hideous?"

Rose looked at Emily. "I can't believe you just through me under the bus like that, and to think I was about to take you with me into town and get a pedi, and I was going to let you drive the Jeep."

Both were laughing now as I was walking away to get a shower.

Emily was playfully begging for Rose's forgiveness. "Please let me drive."

Couldn't believe my baby is old enough to get her driver's license. God help us all.

Needless to say, I couldn't nap. Instead, I went over the layout of Keifer's house. I wanted to go in and just exterminate him, but I needed to know first if Cindy was there, and if not, then where she was.

I was sitting at the desk, going over the layout, windows and doors, closets, and basement, when Rose walked into the room. She walked up behind me and wrapped her arms around me from behind with her head on my shoulder.

Whispered in my ear, "What are you doing, babe?"

"Just memorizing this for later," I replied.

"Who are you taking with us?" she asked.

"Just you, babe," I answered. "That's all I need—you."

"Rip, I'm not ready to do a mission like this. I don't know if I ever will be," Rose replied, a bit flustered.

"No, Rose," I said. "I'm doing this myself. I just need you to drive and to be there for Cindy if she is there. She's not going to know me. Besides, the rest of the team is not going to be back until tomorrow at the earliest. I'm not waiting. If he has my daughter, I want her back home tonight, whatever it takes."

Rose spun my chair around toward her and got down between my legs and wrapped her arms around me, placing her head in my chest, then held me tight. Then her beautiful blue eyes looked up into mine. "Rip, I want Cindy back almost as much as you do. I just worry. Don't let your rage cloud your judgment and get yourself killed. He's a cop, and you know he's well-armed and trained."

I replied, "And I'm sure he will be expecting me, undoubtedly. He already knows what happened at the island. He's mine, and I own him!"

"I know, Rip, I have your back," Rose replied.

She reached in and softly kissed my lips, and I tenderly touched her jaw and kissed her back. Looked back into her eyes, my heart melting from the love burning from her very soul.

"I love you, Rose, never forget that," I said softly.

* * *

We made our way down into the cave and to the armory, where I suited up in black tactical and slipped on my bulletproof vest. I also wired myself for audio and video recording. I was going after a cop, and when I killed him, I'd undoubtedly have the cops in this town who don't know who and what this snake really was wanting my head on a platter, so I'm going to need evidence, providing if who I really am ever came to light.

I looked at Rose. "Let's go get my baby and bring her home."

We jumped into my Jeep and headed into town, Rose driving. We double-checked our comm system, and I told her to stay away from the house, drop me a block away, then wait for instructions.

"Do not come in for any reason unless I call for you to, no matter what you see or hear, okay?" I asked.

"Okay, Rip," Rose nervously replied. "Please be careful, babe. I just have a bad feeling."

I leaned in and kissed her perfect lips. "I will, Rose."

Knowing that he had just gotten off duty, I wasn't surprised that his partner was still there when I arrived. I hid out in the brush, watching and listening with a directional surveillance mic. I could hear plenty of static, but I could hear their conversation—mostly work related, also talking about the receptionist at the chief's office that Keifer was apparently banging behind locked doors. Occasionally I thought I could hear a child's whimper faintly but wasn't positive. I knew he didn't have a child of his own at home, but then again, it could have been a dog, just too faint to know for sure. His wife wasn't home yet and was out playing bridge with the girls and wasn't due home for at least another two hours. By then, this would all be over, one way or the other.

After some time, his partner finally left, and the only sounds I could hear was him messing around in the kitchen, apparently fixing himself something to eat. Knowing where the cameras and motion sensors were located, I worked my way through the yard, avoiding them as much as possible and skillfully moving past the motion sensors without setting them off.

Finally, I got to the back side of the house to the basement window that I had planned on going through to get in. Figuring that if Cindy was there it was likely that she would be kept in the basement, and I wanted to try and find her first before I deal with him.

I switched on my tactical hearing device, which amplifies my hearing capabilities six time over. I listened closely before reaching into my belt and pulling out the suction cup and sticking it on the window square. I then got out the diamond-tipped glass cutter and carefully began cutting out the window square and quietly removing the window and setting it off to the side on the ground. Then I slipped a piece of foil into the window frame where the alarm contact was completing the circuit.

Reaching in, I got ahold of the latch and gently opened the window. Listening, I could still here him fumbling around upstairs. Looking in below the window, I reached in and removed a few things off a table so as to not knock them over. Then slowly I crawled in and lowered myself on to the table then to the floor.

Very nice basement, well-furnished and decorated, way above the means that a sergeant could be making. There were four doors off the room that I was in. I worked my way to the first door and gently tried the knob. The door opened, and I cautiously peered into the room. I cleared it and moved to the next. Tried that door, opening it slowly and peering inside. Then I moved to the third door and tried it. It was locked, and my blood ran cold.

He's hiding something in here.

I pulled out my lockpicks, put the flashlight in my mouth, and quietly worked the lock, clicking tumblers quickly, unlocking the door. I slowly opened the door and peered inside, and there on the bed I could see a lump of blankets.

Slowly I approached the bed and now could plainly see a young child sound asleep. I pulled back the blanket and looked into the face of my girl.

It was Cindy.

Every emotion ran through my heart and mind in a flash. I quickly cupped my hand over her mouth so she wouldn't scream when I would awake her. But she didn't respond; she didn't wake up. I checked her vitals. She was breathing, and she had a pulse. The son of a b——tch had her sedated.

Well, I thought, *it's probably best because now she won't see what I'm going to do to this bastard.*

I said, "Rose?"

She replied on the comm, "Go ahead, Rip, I can hear you."

"I have her, I have Cindy," I replied.

"Oh my god!" Rose cried. "Oh my god." Her voice was breaking as she sobbed.

"He has her heavily sedated, but she seems to be fine," I said. "She's out cold and unaware of anything the best I can tell. Listen closely: I'm going to set her outside the window on the southeast corner of the house that I showed you that I was going to enter the house in, but do not come after her yet. You will trigger his alarms and cameras if you do. Wait until I signal you to come and get her, then get her in the car with you. Okay?"

"Okay, Rip, I'll get her," she answered. "What's going to be the signal?"

"When you hear me blow his head off," I replied.

"Okay," she quietly replied. "Please be careful."

Quietly I picked up and held my baby close in my arms and walked to the window and laid her on the ground, gently brushing her hair back from her little face as I wiped a tear off my cheek. "Daddy loves you with all his heart. You're going to be all right now. Daddy's going to take care of the monster."

I gently kissed her face and turned toward the stairs as my heart turned to fire and ice. Stealthily, I approached the stairs and went up, as I could still hear him in the kitchen at the top of the stairs. With my 9 mm in my hand, I kicked the door open to see Kiefer jumping in total shock, reaching for his service weapon.

I shot his hand, as he screamed obscenities out of pain and his blood splattered on the wall. His eyes were wide in pain and surprise, looking at me, sputtering out, "Who the hell are you?"

"What's wrong? You don't recognize me?" I asked.

Squinting his eyes at me. "No. Am I supposed to?" he replied, holding his hand or what was left of it. "I'm a police officer. You break into my house and shoot me. This is not going to end well for you, motherf——cker."

"Well, at least I don't do little kids, and you never will again," I replied.

He looked past me at the stairway, then back at me.

"My baby is safe now!" I told him.

His eyes got wide as he looked at me in horror. "Rip?" he asked. "Oh my god, is that you? Thank God. I was able to save Cindy from the clutches of being sent to the island like Emily was."

"Shut up, Keifer!" I yelled. "Don't try to play me, you are a lying piece of sh——t! You are behind everything that happened to my family, and now you're going to pay dearly for this and what you've done to my girls and Crystal!"

He looked back at me with a smug look on his face. "Your wife was a little whore!" he yelled. "You should be thankful that I shot her right between the eyes and her friend that came in to try to help. I knew you would show up sooner or later, but I didn't expect you this soon."

Quickly, he grabbed an iron skillet off the burners and threw it at me. As I dodged it, he rushed me, tackling me. We were wrestling and fighting on the floor, and he was trying to disarm me with his good hand. I landed several good blows to his face with my leather gloves on, ripping into his skin. He managed to pull his baton from its holster and brought it across my neck, pinning me to the floor and choking me close to unconsciousness. I managed to reach the hot iron skillet on the floor. I grabbed its handle, laid it right across his face with a smashing blow, burning his skin like bacon.

He was screaming, holding his face, falling off me as I hit him again with it on the other side of his face, knocking him out cold. Standing up and looking down at him, I grabbed him and threw him over my shoulder and carried him into his study, putting him in a barstool, and moved him close to his bar.

"Castration time, a——hole," I said.

I hastily unzipped his trousers and whipped out his wiener. And nailed it to the bar, blood squirting everywhere. Still slumped over, he jerked and came around, screaming at the top of his lungs as I stood back and watched him in so much agonizing pain that he began throwing up on himself.

While he was rather incapacitated, I stepped back into the kitchen and grabbed a butter knife and began beating the edge of it on the cast iron skillet, dinging up the cutting edge and making it jagged. Then I walked back into the study and handed him the knife, saying, "You molested my girls, you bastard, and I intended on killing you, but I think better of it. You are going to castrate yourself with that."

"No, I'm not," he blurted out. "And you certainly can't make me!"

I stopped and looked at him and said, "Really, I can't?"

I began looking around at his selection of alcohol. "Some pretty strong stuff you have here, Keifer. I'll bet this would burn good." I picked up a bottle of 151 off the shelf and looked around the all-wood room while unscrewing the cap.

"What are you doing, Rip?" he asked with a tinge of panic in his voice.

I walked up with the now-open bottle and looked into his eyes as I splashed a little 151 on his wiener, and he began screaming again.

"Oh, damn, that's gotta hurt, huh?" I asked. I then began splashing it around the bar, leaving a trail around where he was. "What am

I going to do? I'm going to light this. The fire is going to spread, so you will either have to cut yourself loose or you will burn alive. Either way, it's going to hurt like hell, so are you sure I can't make you do it?"

I got a book of matches out from behind the bar, and he had a panicked look in his eyes as I struck a match and held it in my fingers, looking at it until it went out. I threw it down and tore another out of the book and struck it and turned toward him.

"What will it be?" I asked.

"I'm not doing it!" he screamed in a very tortured voice.

"Then die," I said.

I threw the match, and it started burning, and I began walking away. Keifer began cussing at me and screaming as the fire spread quickly.

Just as I reached the doorway, he screamed at me. "That's right, you bastard! I had your precious little girl, and you know what? She was good too." He started laughing hysterically.

It was more than I could stand. I reached to my side and drew my Desert Eagle 50 cal, spun, and fired, totally turning his head into a splattering red mist.

"I guess you were right, Keifer," I said. "I couldn't make you castrate yourself."

I turned and walked out of the room and then out of the house, as it was now burning behind me.

I saw Rose running toward me with panic in her eyes.

I asked, "You get Cindy?"

She replied, "Yes."

She drew her gun and aimed it toward me and fired, just as I felt and saw my shoulder splatter in front of me, as I spun and heard another shot as I lost consciousness.

CHAPTER 12

There were sirens and yelling, bright lights, people yelling, pain, oh my god the pain, everything blurry, bright lights in my eyes, someone yelling "Rip!"

What the hell is going on? Where am I? What happened? So confused.

"Stay with me, Rip, stay with me!"

Tasted blood. Coughed up blood. Something over my face. Couldn't breathe. Fading out, what the hell.

Beep, beep, beep, beep. What in the hell was beeping? Annoying when your head was throbbing. Where was I? Couldn't move, couldn't open my eyes. Someone was with me, holding my wrist and my hand.

Am I dead? Why can't I move? Rose? Okay, okay, I remember Rose. Well, yeah, dumbass, she shot you. What the hell? Why did Rose shoot me?

Oh my god, Rose was trying to kill me! Why? Did she hate me? Did I make her coffee wrong? I didn't understand, I told them to put in eight creamers. Sh——t.

My head was spinning from the pain, felts like my shoulder was on a chopping block, very sharp-shooting pain. Moaning. Was that me moaning? Why did Rose shoot me?

Fading out.

Someone lying beside me. *Who's holding me?*

Beep, beep, beep, beep.

Drifting in and out of consciousness. A man's voice talking to me. "Rip, can you hear me? This is Dr. Feldman."

"Daddy, please wake up, Daddy."

Cindy? Is that my Cindy? Her face on my arm. Tears. Are those tears I feel on my arm?

Someone holding my hand. "Rip, baby, please come back to me."

Rose? Why was she crying? Why would she want me to come back? So she could shoot me again?

"Come on, babe, I know you're in there, we need you."

"Dad, please."

Emily?

"Rip, you need to go back, our girls need you there."

Crystal? Oh my god. I am dead, Crystal, I'm sorry.

I could see Crystal's face clearly looking at me, saying, "Go, Rip. The girls need you more than ever now, and so does Rose. It's not your time yet."

I felt a soft, tender kiss on my lips. Felt sparks. Rose. It's my Rose.

I managed to open an eye and slightly move my finger on the hand that was holding mine.

"Daddy! Daddy moved! Daddy!" Cindy was now crying and holding me. I knew you'd come back, I knew it! Oh, Daddy, I love you." She sobbed.

"Rip, can you hear me, babe?" Rose asked. "Come on, babe. Emily, go get the doctor, he's right down the hall, hurry! Cindy, let the doctor in there, honey."

"Rip! This is Dr. Feldman. Can you hear me, Rip? Squeeze my hand, Rip, if you can hear me."

My lips were dry, and my throat was sore as hell, but I managed to say, "Doc, the f——cking dead can hear you. Use your indoor voice, please, I have a hell of a hangover."

The room erupted into laughter. There was a bright light in my eye and then my other eye, but I couldn't see anything but shadows. Everything was blurry but very slowly coming into focus. The doctor was checking my vitals and poking and probing.

Cindy was back at my side, holding my arm. "I knew you would come and rescue us, Daddy. I knew it. Oh, Daddy, I've missed you so much."

There were tears running down my face. I think they were mine. "I love you, girls," I said.

Then Dr. Feldman said, "Okay, ladies. He needs to rest. You go on home and come back in the morning. We are going to run some tests on him."

They were not happy about that, but they came up and kissed me one at a time.

Rose came to me last. She looked down at me and smiled her award-winning smile and bent to kiss me. I was hesitant but returned the kiss.

"I love you, Rip. I'll see you in the morning." She squeezed my hand and walked away.

Looking up at the doc, I asked, "How long have I been out?"

"Going on three weeks," he replied.

"Three weeks? What the hell?"

"You were in pretty bad shape when you came in," he replied.

Just then Boomer came walking into the room. "Well, good morning, Sleeping Beauty," he said.

The doc continued, "We had to completely replace your shoulder. You had a collapsed lung and total cardiac arrest, and you have two cracked ribs in your back. Had it not been for the quick actions of your girlfriend, you wouldn't be here right now."

Looked at Boomer, feeling a little puzzled. "What happened to me, Boomer?" I asked.

Boomer stepped up as the doctor retreaded and headed for the door, saying to Boomer, "Keep it short, he needs to rest."

"Okay, Doc, thank you," Boomer replied.

The doctor went out the door, and I looked up at Boomer. "What the hell happened out there, Boomer? The last thing I remember was Rose shooting at me. I'm confused."

Looking a little bewildered, Boomer said, "Rip, she didn't shoot you."

"Yes, she did. I saw her shoot me in the shoulder. Look at the body cam!"

"Rip, I did, multiple times," he replied.

"Then what happened? If she didn't shoot me, then who did?" I asked.

"Mrs. Keifer shot you, Rip, and Rose shot her."

"Where the hell did she come from? She wasn't there."

"She got home early. That's why Rose came running. You weren't answering your comm, so Rose came running to stop her. She shot you in the shoulder and in the back, and Rose shot and killed her. Hell, Rip, she emptied the clip into that pig."

Slightly at a loss for words, I replied, "Rose did? Rose killed her?"

"Rip, she saved your life, then she saved your life again by performing mouth to mouth and CPR on you until the EMS got there." Boomer looked at me. "We thought we lost you, buddy. A couple of times, it was touch and go. Rose has been by your side continuously almost the whole time. She even crawled in bed with you, not only because she missed you but so she could feel any sign of movement.

"Peyton made her leave after the first week so she could get a shower and sleep while Peyton stayed with you, then Aubrey and she took turns whenever they could get Rose to leave. I'm going to get out of here, and you need to rest buddy. Welcome back. The team sends their best, and by the way, those two goons outside your door are FBI. Officially you are in custody, but SA Blye says he's got you covered. You are being protected. We obviously pissed off a lot of people."

"Well, do me a favor, Boomer," I said. "Make sure these agents are well fed and taken care of when they are here. We are taking care of them."

"Will do, buddy. Listen, I'm out of here. Get some rest, and I'll see you soon. You behave."

We both chuckled, and he walked out the door, greeting the agents.

The next morning, I woke up to the strong aroma of coffee. Before even opening my eyes, I knew it was my Rose. Opening my eyes, I saw her sitting by my side with her head down and her eyes closed and her little hand in mine.

"You know," I said, "I just got back from heaven, and there wasn't a single angel up there that could hold a candle to the angel I have right here."

Her little head raised up, and the brightest blinding smile I'd ever seen brightened up my life. "Good morning, love," she said, as she leaned into me and kissed me. "How are you feeling this morning?"

"Like I've been hit by a truck and had my arm cut off. Other than that, I feel great." I then held her cheek and looked into her blue eyes. "How are you feeling, babe?" I asked softly.

"I'm way better now that you're back," she replied.

She gently laid her head on my chest and sighed. I gently stroked her beautiful hair with my good hand. She reached up and took my hand and whispered, "Just hold me, Rip, just hold me."

I held her the best I could for a little while until a vociferous nurse came walking in with a wheelchair.

"Good morning, sleepyhead," she boomed. "Doc says we need to get you started in therapy this morning. Hope you're ready."

Rose assisted her with getting me in the wheelchair, and the nurse began pushing me out the door, looking back at Rose. "You too, honey, come on now. We need you to kick him when he slacks off." She chuckled.

The two agents followed along as we went down the hall, and they stayed near while I was in therapy for the next couple weeks. It was a hard and slow, painful progress, but slowly, day by day, it got a little better. Rose was by my side every step of the way.

A couple at a time, the team made their way up to see me, cracking up and joking—anything to keep my spirits up. Enjoyed our one-on-one time. They really are a great team.

The doctor came in and did his examination on me and read the assessment from therapy and said, "Rip, you are making great progress. I don't see any reason that you can't go home today. Just follow up with therapy twice a week. Don't overdo it with that shoulder, but keep it moving."

I looked over at Rose then at the doc. "I'm planning on a vacation here very soon, Doc. Will there be any problem with missing about two weeks of therapy?" Looked back at Rose, who had a questioning look on her face.

"I don't see why not, Rip," the doctor said. "Again, just don't overdo it, and keep doing your exercises and stretches, and you will be fine."

"Great," I replied, as I reached out and shook his hand. "Thank you."

"No, Rip, thank *you* for what you and your team do," the doctor said. "From all of us to all of you, thank you, and it's been an honor."

Rose stepped forward and gave him a hug and thanked him as well.

Rose and I began gathering my things as she phoned Peyton to have her bring the car around to pick us up. I changed my sweats into street clothes, and the nurse brought in a second wheelchair to load with the flowers and stuff.

The agents stepped into the door, and one of them said, "We will be following you back to your compound and leaving you at your gate, and you will be on your own. Also, thank you for your hospitality, making sure we were taken care of."

Shaking their hands, I replied, "We're in this together, guys. Thank you."

Rose looked at me and asked, "Vacation?"

I just gave her a smile and replied, "Yes, love, vacation."

"Where are we going?" she asked.

"How does Maui, Hawaii, sound to you?"

"Oh, Rip, really?" Rose asked excitedly.

"Yes, the whole team is going on vacation, God knows they've earned it, but no worries, you and I will have plenty of alone time, just you and I."

"Oh my god, my toes are a mess." She looked at her hands. "And my nails. I can't go like this, Rip," she said in a slightly panicked voice.

Laughing at her sweetness, I replied, "You and Peyton and Aubrey and the girls are all going to go shopping and have a spa day."

"When are we going?" she excitedly asked.

"I'm going to make the arrangements tomorrow, and I'll let you know, but don't say a word to anyone."

The nurse returned and asked, "Are you ready to go?"

"Yes," I replied. "I believe we have everything. Let's go home."

As we were going down the hallway, we were greeted by several doctors, nurses, and orderlies bidding us well-wishes and goodbyes, giving us a couple of hugs, and patting our backs. As we approached the front doors, we were met by a smiling Peyton opening the doors to the big black Hummer.

Getting out of the wheelchair, I pulled myself into the back seat, and Rose got in on the other side. The orderly finished loading the stuff into the back and closed the hatch. The agents pulled their black Tahoe in front of us as Peyton fired up the beast, and we rolled out into the street, heading home. Rose and I held hands as we talked to Peyton and got updates on how the bar was doing in Rose's absence. Peyton had a good handle on things.

When we arrived back at the ranch, the agents turned and left us as we entered the driveway. As we pulled in by the house, the front door flew open, and out came Emily and Cindy running and screaming "Dad!" They were followed close behind by Aubrey; she stood on the porch and watched.

I barely got out of the door, and I was being hugged and kissed by my babies, and I held them all so tight. Rose stood near with teary eyes and watched, and she smiled. I stood to my feet and heard a throat being cleared. I turned to see the entire team standing near and watching.

I walked into the group of some of the most amazing men I've ever had the pleasure of knowing. If not for them, my little girls would be gone. After many handshakes and one-armed man hugs, I stepped back with the girls and turned to address everyone. Looked across many smiling faces looking back.

Slightly lost for words, I said, "Thank you. Every single one of you, thank you from the bottom of my heart."

My girls were standing on either side of me with my arms around them, and Rose was behind me with her arms around me.

"I love you, guys, and I respect and appreciate you all. With that said"—I looked around, making sure everyone was present—"we are taking a couple of weeks off for a well-deserved and earned vacation, and I'm buying. Anyone here want to go to Hawaii?"

"Hell, yes!" was the general reply and cheers.

"When are we going?" came a voice from the back. Bull came walking forward through the crowd.

I was rather stunned, as we aren't used to Bull speaking. I replied, "I'm not sure yet. I'll be making the arrangements tomorrow morning, and I'll let you all know as soon as I know."

Looking down, Bull said, "Well, I need to get me a surfboard."

Looked at Boomer in shock, and he returned the look.

"Well, Bull, we didn't know you surfed," I said.

Bull replied, "Well, of course I surf. Chicks dig it!"

Cindy went running up to Bull and looked up at his mountainous frame and asked, "Will you teach me to surf, Mr. Bull?"

Bull looked at me with a panicked, puzzled look on his face. He then looked down into that little face of innocence and knelt down in front of her, still towering over her. He looked back at me as I watched in amazement. "Well, Cindy, if it's okay with your dad, I'd love to teach you."

Cindy looked back at me over her shoulder.

I replied with a straight face, "Of course, Cindy, that's fine."

Cindy, unable to contain herself, screamed and jumped up and down, turning back to Bull, and shr wrapped her arms around his neck. Bull slowly and delicately put his massive arm around Cindy as if he was terrified he was going to break her. He looked at me again as if looking for my permission to hug her. The team, all watching this, began chuckling and was astonished at Bull.

"Gentlemen, if it's all the same to you, I'm going to spend the rest of the day with my family," I said. "I'll be out and about tomorrow. Why don't you guys take the night and just go out and enjoy yourselves? We've got some catching up to do."

The group walked away, talking and planning about what they wanted to do in Hawaii.

Aubrey had dinner ready for us. We sat and ate and chatted around the table. Though the girls appeared to be happy and excited about being home and reunited, I could sense deep emotional turmoil between them, and undoubtedly, it was going to take some time and counseling to address it. But for tonight, it was just the four of us, and I was loving it.

I woke up early the next morning spooning Rose, listening to her soft breathing and gently stroking her hair as she melted into me, and a soft sigh escaped her lips. The warmth of her body against me and feeling her heartbeat made it difficult to get out of bed, but the stiffness was getting overwhelming, and I was going to need to stretch it out, and my shoulder was getting stiff too.

Slowly I pulled away and got out of bed, covering her and tucking her in. I bent and tenderly kissed her hair-covered little face and whispered, "I love you." I went out into the kitchen and set up the coffeepot and turned it on as I knew she would be getting up soon. I then went outside and headed to the bunker. Got to the entrance and used the biometric scanner and scanned my thumbprint for access. Pushed the button on the intercom to the control center and identified myself as the door unlocked, and I walked in and headed down to the long hall.

When I entered the control center, I was greeted by the security officer on duty. I shook his hand and thanked him for keeping an eye on the place and asked him how things were going and if there was anything needed or should be addressed.

He replied, "No, sir. Boomer takes care of our needs pretty well. We had some bugs to work out of the system, but I think we're in good shape. Nobody can get on to the property without us knowing it instantly."

"That's great," I said. "By the way, I know you guys can't go with us on vacation as this compound cannot be left unsecure, so what I'm going to do, you each are going to receive a significant bonus plus a two-week paid vacation to wherever you and your families want to go. It'll have to be scheduled."

"Thank you so much, sir," he said. "I can't tell you how much that'll mean to us."

"You guys are a part of the team," I answered. "We depend on you and your department to keep us all safe on our downtime. I'm going to use this station over here to make our vacation arrangements. I'll try not to be in your way."

"You won't be in my way, boss, it's all yours."

I sat down at the computer and started planning for our trip, along with an incredibly special surprise. Ten days and nights on Maui—all inclusive, a private beach luau, parasailing, with many other little excursions that Hawaii has to offer. A private plane will be chartered to take the entire team. This was going to be a great time.

After making the arrangements, I went back up topside, heading toward the house, and there was my angel drinking her coffee, the sun glistening off her coal-black hair and her smile.

As I approached, she reached down and handed me a cup of coffee. "I figured you wouldn't be long," she said, as she kissed me.

"Well, it's set," I said. "We leave for Maui in a week."

"Oh, Rip!" she replied excitedly. "A week isn't much time."

"Well, you better get busy." I chuckled.

We sat holding hands, and I filled her in on the arrangements.

She said, "Well, I'll get the girls together, and we are going to hit the salon today and do some shopping. We need clothes and swimsuits. The kids need everything."

Handing her my card, I replied, "Here you go. You get whatever you need and have a great time. I have got some shopping to do myself. I'll see you back here later, okay? By the way, Rose, what do you think about building us a house here on the ranch. This is Boomer's home. I think we need a place of our own now that we have the girls back."

With a glimmer in her eyes and a smile, she replied, "I was just thinking about how to ask you that very thing myself. Yes, I agree we should."

"Okay, love, you've got it," I replied. "Log home?"

"Oh my god, yes, please!"

"Okay, we'll plan it when we get back." I kissed her and said, "You guys better get started. You have a full day ahead."

She got the girls up, and they all headed into town, taking two security escorts with them just for safety's sake. And myself, I had my own secret shopping to do.

This was going to be epic!

CHAPTER 13

The ladies were pulling out of the driveway as Boomer came walking from the barn.

"How are you feeling today, Rip?" he asked.

Pulled my arm out of the sling, and I slowly rubbed it, moving it around and stretching it.

"It's stiff and sore, but it's functional," I replied. I handed Boomer the printouts of the itinerary of the vacation. "Here's copies for everyone, if you would distribute them, so they can plan accordingly."

Boomer looked them over. "In a week?" he asked.

"That's not much time, but it's much needed by all of us."

Then he looked at me. "Let's go for a ride, Rip. I have a couple of horses saddled up."

"Great, let's go," I replied.

We walked down to the barn where two beauties were saddled and tied to the post. I reached down and untied mine, and with some difficulty, I managed to get up on her back.

"Boomer," I said, "Rose and I are talking about building a house so we can let you have your home back to yourself. What are your thoughts?"

As Boomer swung his leg over his horse as he mounted, he looked back at me and replied, "Brother, there is no hurry, but yes, of course. Are you planning on staying here on the ranch?"

We began steering the horses out of the corral.

"Yes," I said. "As we move along in this mission, we are going to need the protection of this compound, especially should anyone get wind of who we are and where we are."

"Agreed," Boomer replied. "Do you have a site in mind, Rip, that you want to build on?"

"Yes, I do, but I want to show it to Rose and make sure it's okay with her before we decide," I replied. "But we can ride out there and get your thoughts on it."

"Okay, let's go," he replied.

I brought the horse into a gallop toward the woods, with Boomer by my side. It felt so good to be riding free with the wind in my face. We approached the back forty, where there was somewhat of a clearing in the woods. Quiet and peaceful yet close to the compound.

"This is the spot I'm thinking, Boomer," I said. "I think Rose and the girls will agree. We are going with a log home. When we return from vacation, I think we are going to make a trip down to Missouri to a place I know that custom builds real log homes from real logs. They build on their grounds, number the logs, disassemble it, then reassemble it where we want it. Beautiful homes, solid thick walls, and efficient. I figured we could go with solar panels on the roof with a backup solar tree with a 5,000 w windmill on the top. Run an underground tunnel into the compound from the basement. Interlink the compound power grid to ours so we would act as a backup power source for the compound and vice versa. What do you think?"

Boomer was deep in thought, and looking around. He turned to me and replied, "That's a great idea, and this is all still inside of our sensors, although we should probably extend it a little farther in this area just for safety's sake."

Nodding my head in agreement, I replied, "Absolutely. I'll bring my queen out here and see what she thinks."

Boomer then looked at me and said, "Rip, I want to run this by you and see what you think. SA Blye says he will supply us with whatever we need to complete our missions. Obviously they are going to run us all over the country, and we need stuff to be effective. We need rolling command centers and equipment. I drew up a set of plans and ideas I want to run by you. Right now, no one knows about this but you and I."

Looking at Boomer, I replied, "What do you have?"

Reaching into his saddlebag, he pulled out an aluminum clipboard, opened it, pulled out papers with drawings and notes, and handed them to me. "And we're going to have to bring on more manpower to man this equipment."

Shuffling through the papers and studying the diagrams, I looked at Boomer. "In your words, what are you thinking, Boomer? I'm seeing some serious firepower in these things. Very impressive."

"Well," Boomer replied, "start out with, this semi will be armored front to back and top to bottom. We'll use a 53 feet and 108 inch wide double-drop trailer with a rear door ramp set up for rapid rolling deployment of these armored battle buggies. Above the battle buggies will be a drone-swarm launch area with the roof sliding open. In the double-drop area, on the lower level, the sides will open into ramps on both sides for the four wheelers to deploy. The center will be the storage area.

"The upper level will be the berthing area for the teams. The neck area in front will be the control center and armory. The trailer will be equipped with four remote laser-guided mini guns that can work autonomously if needed to protect our perimeter. Each one of our team members will always be equipped with transponders that will identify themselves as friendlies, so as if the guns are set up autonomously, they will not accidently be shot.

"The tractor will be armored also, along with a solid steel bumper brush guard to protect the entire front end from and impacts up to and including mowing through vehicles and buildings. The control center will be escorted by two armored H1 Hummers, also with solid bumpers. All vehicles will have airless puncture-proof tires. Both Hummers will be armed with a mini hydra rocket pod. Also, an M134 minigun 7.62. These will be controlled by the passenger wearing a HUDS helmet. Both weapons will retract down into the Hummer when not in use."

Looked over the diagrams and listening to Boomer. It was quite an impressive presentation. "Do you think SA Blye will go along with this?" I asked.

Boomer, looking hopeful, replied, "I hope so, Rip, because I want two sets for two teams. We can split up and cover more, and if we have a bigger job, we can team up.

"Well, I like it. When do you want to present this to him?" I asked.

"As soon as possible," he replied. "Preferably before we leave for vacation. I'm already putting together the specs to give him."

"Okay, we will set up a meeting the day before we leave for Maui if SA Blye is available," I replied. "Meantime, I have to go shopping. This will be a great time."

Boomer looked at me and said, "You have something special planned, Rip?"

I just replied with a grin and turned toward the horses.

Boomer, laughing, said, "I thought so."

He chuckled, and we mounted up and headed back.

After putting up the saddles and brushing down the horses and while turning them loose in the coral I asked Boomer, "You want to ride into town with me? Since I should have a bodyguard with me as I'm not fully functional yet. You would be the best man for the job."

"I would like to, Rip, but I need to get this put together. I'll get Bull to go with you," he replied. He pulled his phone out and called Bull. "Bull, you think you could ride into town with Rip for a little bit? Thanks."

Boomer hung up, smiling, and looked at me. "He just grunted."

Laughing, I replied, "A man of few words, but he surprises us sometimes. I think Cindy has him wrapped around her finger."

Boomer said, "I believe you're right. This will be interesting to watch, Bull on a surfboard."

We were chuckling as Bull came walking up to us. We'd take the Hummer as Bull wouldn't fit in the Jeep.

Driving into town, we approached a CPD cruiser with a car stopped. I swerved out from the vehicles to allow for safety, being as we couldn't see anyone. As we went around, I glanced over and could see the officer and suspect rolling on the ground and a second suspect exiting the vehicle, appearing to be going back to assist the first guy. I rapidly pulled over, and Bull and I jumped out of the Hummer and ran back toward the scene just as we heard a shot, then a second. The second suspect was jumping into the driver's seat and speeding away, as the first perp saw us and turned to fire at us.

I pulled my weapon and fired two rounds into the center torso and one to the head. Bull turned and ran back to the Hummer, saying, "I'll get him," as the car sped away. Bull was in hot pursuit.

I ran to the officer on the ground and knelt by his side. "I've got you, brother, I've got you."

He was bleeding pretty bad from a neck wound, and it appeared that his vest had stopped the first round, though he was in pain and jerking and groaning as I applied direct pressure on his neck. I grabbed the microphone on his vest and keyed up, saying, "Officer down. I repeat, officer down. Send wagon and send help. Suspect has been exterminated, and second suspect drove off, but my partner is in pursuit eastbound from this location on Fifth Avenue."

Dispatch replied, "What is the condition of the officer?"

I replied, "He is wounded and down. His vest stopped one round, and he is bleeding from the neck. I'm applying pressure, but I don't think it's enough. Get help here fast, he is currently conscious."

"Help is en route," dispatch replied. "Identify yourself."

Ignored the request from dispatch. I could hear the multiple sirens approaching.

"Stay with me, brother," I said. "Help is almost here. Hang on, you'll be fine."

Looking back up at me with fear in his wide eyes, he tried to speak. "Tell my wife and kids—"

I stopped him short, saying, "You tell them yourself. You stay with me, you hear me?"

The EMS pulled up as the CPD did, and everyone jumped into action, grabbing equipment from the wagon and running to us and taking over, pushing me back out of the way. The sergeant led me away from the scene. "What the hell happened?" he asked.

I told him step by step what took place that I had seen and up to present. "You should have caught it on the dash cam."

The one paramedic approached us and said to the sergeant, "The shooter is dead from multiple gunshot wounds."

Just then Bull pulled up in the Hummer with the second suspect tied to the hood of the Hummer as if he was a prize-hunting trophy.

"What in the hell?" the sergeant said in utter disbelief.

"The second suspect," I replied, chuckling at Bull as he got out and untied him for the awaiting officers.

The sergeant looked at me and Bull and asked, "Who are you guys?"

Then I heard a voice coming from behind us, saying, "Aren't you Rip?"

I turned to see a lieutenant approaching us. "Yes, you are. You're the guy that killed Sergeant Keifer a few weeks ago and his wife."

Now every officer was turning their attention toward us and approached us. I could plainly see these officers were upset about this.

The lieutenant spoke up. "We don't like cop killers, Rip, not at all. The only thing we hate more than cop killers are pedophiles, though. Under the circumstances, well, I can't condone what you did. At the same time, I can't say that I blame you either. I know that you are under some sort of federal contract, so I guess all I can say is thank you for saving this officer's life, and I hope that in the future we can work together." He looked up at Bull. "And you too." Chuckling, he looked back at me. "What the hell do you feed this guy?"

Laughingly, I replied, "Anything he wants, Lieutenant. Anything he wants."

After filling out written statements on the incident, we were released to go on our way.

* * *

Finally, it was the day before we were to leave for vacation, and the ranch was bustling with anticipation. The girls were so excited they could barely maintain themselves, although Emily seemed a bit off. Though she was excited, something was definitely bothering her.

I caught ahold of her alone and said, "Hey, beautiful, what's going on?"

She looked back at me quickly then looked away from my eye contact and replied, "Nothing, Daddy, just trying to pack for tomorrow."

Well, I knew my baby: when she looks away from eye contact and says nothing, I know she's lying. I didn't want to press the issue right now. She'd been through a lot, but I will when we get back.

Rose and I were in our room packing, and she was asking my opinion on different outfits. I was laughing to myself at first then out loud, and said, "Baby, we're not moving there permanently, just for ten days."

She looked at me as if I had just killed the cat. "It's going to take twelve hours to get there, so that's at least one outfit. Then no less than two outfits per day, three to play it safe, and then special events, a couple more outfits. So safe to say, at least thirty-five to forty outfits." Then she smiled. "Plus shoes." She gave me her best stunning ear-to-ear smile and got back to packing.

Now I was laughing. "Okay, babe, I'm thinking I'm just going to pack like Bull is packing," I replied.

"What is he taking?" she asked.

"Well, I talked to him earlier, and he's just carrying a shoulder satchel with a T-shirt and a pair of Speedos," I replied, laughing.

Rose froze and turned and looked at me like I had killed the cat's kittens. "You are not, and oh my god, Bull in a Speedo?"

I was laughing at her reaction and replied, "I'm joking, Rose. I'm packed for the days we're there plus a couple of extra items."

"Hey, Rip, are you in here?" I heard Boomer's voice.

"Yes, come in, Boomer," I replied.

He walked in.

"How did the meeting go with SA Blye this morning?" I asked.

"Well, he seemed to be in complete agreement with us, and he said he'll see what we can put together. I gave him the complete shopping list and the specs, and now we'll see."

Rose looking at me quizzically.

"I'll fill you in on the flight, lover," I said." We are taking all the luggage to the airport tonight and load the plane so all we have to do in the morning is get our asses to the airport by 0600, so make sure all of your bags are tagged, and I'll let the girls know also. Are you packed, Boomer?"

"Buddy, I've been ready for a couple of days," he replied.

"Well, let's get the Hummers loaded up," I said. "Let the team know. Make sure our equipment and weapons are loaded onto the plane also, just in case. You never know."

The sun was beginning to set, and Rose and the kids loaded up in the open Jeep, and we drove out across the fields, taking them to the proposed site of where I wanted to build the house. We arrived at the base of the wooded hill, where we stopped and looked the site over as I pointed out my vision of our homestead.

Rose was leaning over to me and hugging my arm with her head on my shoulder, and said, "I love it, babe. What do you think, girls?"

"Can we have a dog and a horse here, Dad?" asked Cindy.

"I don't see why not. What do you think, Emily?"

"Yeah, sure," she replied unenthusiastically.

"Would you rather a different place or arrangement, Emily?" I asked.

"No, this is fine," Emily replied.

I looked back at Emily into her eyes and said, "Hey, Emily, I love you."

Instantly, tears welled up in her eyes.

"Forever in a day. Remember that."

Rose looked back at both girls and said, "I love you both as if you were my own, and I'm here for you no matter what."

Cindy smiled her biggest smile and replied, "We're here for you too, no matter what. Aren't we, Em?"

"Yup," Emily replied.

We drove back to the ranch in silence. Upon arrival, the girls got out and ran to the house as Rose and I got out and held hands walking out to the gazebo. The stars were out shining brightly, and we stood leaning into each other with our arms around each other's backs and my hand on her perfectly shaped firm little ass. We stood staring at the beautiful sky for a couple of minutes.

Rose said, "Rip, I love you with all of my heart and soul."

We turned toward each other, my arms around her back and her arms around my neck, her looking up at me. The moon and the stars shone onto her gorgeous face, and I was in awe that such a goddess could ever love a man like me, but here we were, and I was mesmerized by her, as her eyes were brighter than all the stars in the sky.

"I love you more," I replied.

I leaned down, and we kissed slowly and deeply.

CHAPTER 14

Morning came, and chaos ensued in the household, as expected, as the girls ran about trying to get ready, tripping and bumping into each other. Until I reminded them it was a twelve-hour flight and they could get ready on the plane, then everyone was much calmer.

"Okay, ladies, let's go," I said. "The team is already at the airport waiting for us."

Rose, Peyton, and Aubrey loaded up in one Hummer, and the kids and I loaded up in the other, and we headed to the airport. We headed down the driveway, and the girls were chatting away about what they wanted to do and see. Right in the middle of the discussion, Cindy turned to me and asked, "Dad, is Rose our mom now?"

Caught off guard, I replied, "Well, no, not yet. Would you like her to be?"

Their faces both looked at me with wide eyes.

"Well, yes, kind of, but what about Mom?" Emily replied. "I miss her really bad, and I feel like I'd be betraying her, Dad."

I reached over and took Emily by the hand. "Girls, your mother would want you two to be happy, and, well, your mother loved Rose, and Rose loved her, and your mother knew that Rose loved and treated you girls like her own. That made your mom very happy. Rose will never replace your mom, and she would never try to, but she will be a mother figure to you. She loves you very much."

"Are you going to ask her to marry you, Dad?" Cindy asked, as she held my arm and smiled at me.

Chuckling, I replied, "When the time is right, I just might. How's that? Would that be okay with you girls if I did?"

Cindy's gleaming big smile, as she excitedly replied, "Hell, yes, it's okay with me. How about you, Em?"

Instantly, Cindy realized she had cussed. Her eyes flew open in panic, and her hand went over her mouth, and she looked at me in horror, waiting for a scolding. Emily's mouth was partially open in surprise as she looked at me and then Cindy.

I smiled and said, "It's okay, you were excited, and it just slipped out. Just don't make a habit of it." I reached over with one arm and hugged her and touched Emily's face. "What do you say we head to Maui?"

In agreement, we turned into the airport and headed to our gate, where the private jet awaited. The girls were just parking as we pulled in beside them, and we headed to the plane. The team was already on board, and the engines began firing up as we approached the stairs. The guys already had made themselves at home. They had the TV on and were watching the game and enjoying snacks and drinks.

I went to the cockpit and met the pilots and exchanged pleasantries and then headed back into the spacious cabin. I greeted the team and joked with them a bit and then informed them we would be stopping briefly in Denver to refuel. I went back to the next cabin and made myself comfortable, settling in beside a smiling Rose. Kissing her sweet face and watching the girls fussing with their bags. Peyton and Aubrey were seated and chatting up a storm.

It was a long flight. We slept, we ate, we talked. I filled them in on what the meeting with SA Blye was about and what it all meant. I filled in Rose on the conversation I had with the girls on the way to the airport, and tears welled up in her blue eyes as she looked at the now-sleeping girls.

Looking at me, Rose said, "Oh, Rip, I do love them as if they were mine, but I'd never try to replace Crystal."

"I know that, babe. It'll be fine. They've been through hell, and you and those two incredible women"—I motioned toward Peyton and Aubrey—"are instrumental parts of their recovery."

Rose looking into my eyes in silence then, as if she was waiting for me to say something. I only replied with a hug, planting a kiss on her forehead, and whispered into her ear, "When the time is right, love."

* * *

Rose was sound asleep and the girls were playing cards as I sat with Aubrey and Peyton. I filled them in on the planned activities and the secret activity I had planned as a surprise, and they were both sworn to secrecy until the right time.

The pilot came on the intercom and said, "We are in a holding pattern around the Maui airport in line for landing, and we should be landing shortly. Please be seated and buckled in."

My phone rang, and I saw that it was Special Agent Blye. I answered, "Yes, sir."

Special Agent Blye replied, "Have you been watching the news over in Denver?"

"No, I haven't, I'm on vacation. What's going on?"

"So apparently, a local ut job was shot by the police, and the tensions are running pretty high. Nuts Lives Matter is pressing for civil unrest if this officer isn't prosecuted. You know as well as I do that it's not going to matter what the verdict is with this shooting. They're going to riot."

"It's never about justice, it's about raising tensions and dividing the country," I stated. "What does this have to do with us?"

"Just stay aware, Rip. The governor and the mayor are both flaming idiots, and they're already caving to these terrorist demands. But the powers that be higher up don't want this to get out of control. Intervention may be required."

"Well, riots are kind of out of our spectrum though, SA Blye," I replied. "Besides, my guys have earned this vacation. We'll see how things look in ten days."

"Agreed, Rip. I'm just saying that rules sometimes need to be broken nowadays. I'll talk to you soon, Rip."

Hanging up, I looked over at Rose, who had a concerned look on her face.

"No worries, love," I said. "We are not going to shorten our vacation."

We were circling the Island of Maui, and everyone was peering out the windows at the beautiful sights and at Haleakala, which means "the house of the sun." One of two volcanoes on the island of Maui. It was a very majestic view, and the girls were in awe.

We landed finally and taxied to the private-plane gates, where we were greeted by the native ladies in grass skirts putting beautiful leis around the team's necks, kissing them and welcoming us to the islands. We were met by the hotel manager and his shuttle buses to take us to the hotel right on Kaanapali Beach and where we had an entire floor rented for the duration of our stay.

The ride over was scenic and beautiful. I looked back at Peyton and Aubrey, and the excitement on those beautiful smiling faces was great. Cindy was so excited she couldn't sit still at all, and Emily was excited as well, but I could tell she was trying hard to suppress her excitement. Rose was in awe, but she was dragging her tired ass and couldn't wait to get to the hotel and shower and nap before we went out for dinner tonight.

It was a five-star hotel, and beautiful. The girls had an adjoining room to ours, and when we wanted privacy, all we had to do was flick a button and lock it. The rooms were spacious and tastefully furnished, and the bathrooms were great. Large marble walk-in showers with multiple waterfall showerheads in the ceiling and coming out of the wall on two sides with high water pressure.

Rose and I laid down on the bed beside each other, exhausted. I reached over and gently ran my fingers on her back slowly and teasingly.

"Oh, Rip," she softly said. "You keep doing that, you're going to put me to sleep." She moaned her pleasure. "I'm going to get a shower," she said, turning to me.

I was lying on my side, looking into her eyes, and said, "Thank you."

"For what?" she asked.

"I never thanked you for saving my life at Keifer's," I replied. "You saved me a couple of times over, and I know that was difficult for you to take someone's life like that. I hear you sometimes at night in your sleep, I know you are reliving it."

Rose now had tears in her eyes but was fighting them back and said, "But I'm not sorry I did it, Rip It was either her or you, and I can't lose you again."

I gently brushed her hair back out of her eyes and slowly and tenderly kissed her forehead, as she closed her eyes and wrapped her arms around me.

"I love you, Rose," I said. "You have added love and beauty back into my life that I've never known before."

We laid in each other embrace and basked in each other's love. Until she pulled back and looked into my eyes. "I've got to shower," she said, trotting off to the bathroom.

Now another man might have rolled over and taken a nap while she showered, or another man might have taken off running in behind her to join her, but I'm not another man. I waited a couple of minutes after I heard her get into the shower, and I could hear her verbally yell "We need this shower in our room in our house, Rip!" And then I stripped and ran quietly to the bathroom and quietly opened the door and snuck in.

Rose was standing in all her breathtaking glory in the center of the waterfalls, which were blasting her from all sides, her eyes closed and her face upward as the water poured over her face and body. Definitely a stunning sight to remember.

I slowly walked through the glass doors into this shower with her and walked up behind her just as she said, "I was wondering what was taking you so long." She playfully giggled.

I wrapped my arms around her body from behind and held her close to mine.

"What do you think you're doing there, buster," she asked.

I said, "Nothing." I pulled my hands back, and she quickly grabbed them and held them in place.

"You're not going anywhere," she said.

My head was now looking over her shoulder as my chin was resting on it. I whispered in her ear, "You wanna play, little girl?"

She replied with her soft giggle.

I pulled my head back and asked, "What is this on your shoulder, baby?"

"Where?" she asked, trying to look at the spot I was pointing at.

"Right here." I pointed.

"I don't see anything," she replied. "What is it?"

"It's a freckle," I replied, as I softly kissed it.

"You sh——thead." She sighed.

"You hear that? It's another freckle, saying, in a very small voice, 'What about me, Rip?'" I gently brushed my lips across her shoulder an inch or so and softly kissed another spot.

"You are such a goof," she softly whispered.

Another very small voice. "Me too, Rip, me too." I slowly brushed my lips toward her beautiful neck. Her head slightly tilted to the left as I planted a long soft kiss while breathing light hot air into her neckline. Then I moved to another spot and then another slowly and tenderly. Lifting her long black hair, I moved to the back of her neck as she tilted her head forward.

Then she said, "Did you hear that, Rip?" She pointed to the other side of her neck. "I hear one or two over here calling you." Her head rolled to the right, and I moved to the other side and tenderly kissed a couple of freckles. Her hand came up and gently held my head as her breathing increased.

"Oh, God, Rip," she said, as she turned completely around, facing me with her arms around my neck. I held her close to me. Looking into my eyes, she whispered, "What's going on down there, mister?"

"I don't know, what's going on down there?"

She leaned in, and we deeply and softly kissed with great passion. Our hands found each other's hands, and our fingers interlocked as I moved forward, moving her backward to the shower wall. I then hastily brought her hands up and spread her arms, pinning her to the wall. She looked at me with surprise. I moved her hands to the grab handles on the shower wall and making her hold them as if she were tied in place.

"What are you up to, buster?" she asked excitedly.

"Don't you hear that choir of little freckles calling for attention, babe?"

She replied with a slow *yes* nod, as I moved into her neck and began kissing one spot and then another. Her breathing became a little more erratic as I ever so slowly moved down and across her shoulders and arms. Then the front of her shoulders from one side to the other, teasingly but not directly brushing against her perfect breasts. Her breathing got heavier as I moved down to her belly, kissing and brushing across it gently and slowly moving down more.

I looked up into her blue eyes peering down at me as she said in a soft barely audible whisper, "You're killing me, lover."

I smiled up at her and moved down directly to her thighs as she moaned out her frustration, and I giggled my orneriness. She said, "You are such an ass."

Still holding on to those handles, she looked like a prisoner of love, and I was enjoying driving her nuts. I began moving back up, kissing around Rose's rose petals, and she now was pushing it out toward me to meet my kisses and gentle licks. Until finally I made direct contact, and Rose shook and quivered and gasped for air. Parting the petals and planting several kisses and licks directly on her rosebud, sending her into convulsions with moans and groans as she shook. I stood up and pinned Rose against the shower wall, and we made mad, passionate love standing up in the shower until we both were spent and exhausted.

I think we may have used up all the hot water, but it was a wonderful shower, and we were drying off as we heard a gentle knock on the door from the girls' room.

"What is it, girls?" I asked.

Cindy's little voice replied, "Dad, can I come in? It's important."

"Just a minute, honey, we're getting dressed," I replied.

Rose went back into the bathroom and shut the door, and I quickly got dressed and opened the door. Cindy's little face was looking up at me with fear in her eyes.

"What's wrong, baby?" I asked, as I knelt down and hugged her tight. "Are you okay?"

She sheepishly nodded her head yes, but her eyes were saying no. Then she said, "Daddy, I don't want to be a tattletale, but I feel that I have to. She's going to be so mad at me."

"Who? Emily?" I asked. "Where is she?"

"She's getting a shower, Dad," she replied.

"Well, what are you tattling about?" I asked.

Cindy reached into her pocket and slowly pulled out a pill bottle. And handed it over to me.

"Where did you get this?" I asked.

"It fell out of Emily's bag when I moved her bag to get my stuff."

I looked at the bottle. The label was clearly removed, and I opened it and looked inside. They looked like my painkillers from my surgeries. I looked into Cindy's eyes, and she was scared and sad.

"I'm sorry, Daddy, I didn't know what to do. She's going to hate me."

"No, baby, I've got you," I replied. I went into their room to Emily's bag.

"Emily," I said through the door.

"I'm almost done, Dad," she replied.

"Okay. I'm helping Cindy get clothes for dinner tonight. Do you know which bag has her good clothes?"

"I think it's the pink bag with Eeyore on it, Dad."

"Okay, thank you," I replied. I knelt down to Cindy. "You go in my room and shut the door. You've never seen anything, okay?"

"Okay, Daddy." Cindy hugged my neck and kissed me and ran to the other room.

I stood up and asked, "Are you excited about the luau tomorrow night, Em?"

She replied, "Oh yes, I can't wait."

"Well, there's a special surprise tomorrow. I sure hope you like it—" Then I stopped talking in midsentence. "Em! What is this!"

"What, Dad?" she replied, as she walked out of the bathroom with her hair wrapped in a towel. She stopped, suddenly frozen with wide eyes, as I stood looking at her with the pill bottle in my hand.

"This fell out of your bag when I grabbed Cindy's bag. What are these?" I asked.

Emily stood there stammering, not knowing what to say. "I found them," she blurted out as she quickly looked away.

"Emily," I said sternly. "Look at me. What are you doing with these?"

She began sobbing. "They're for pain, Dad."

"What kind of pain, baby? Are you hurting?" I asked.

"You wouldn't understand," she replied in a flustered tone.

"Try me, honey. I know you have been through hell and back, and I know there was horrible things done to you," I said, trying to choke back the tears. "Is it the pain of remembering that you are trying to numb or stop?"

She looked up at me with her momma's big eyes and burst into tears. "Oh, Dad," she cried. She wrapped herself around me, and I held her tight with all my might and cried with and for her.

I looked past her, and Rose was standing in the doorway, crying with us silently, and she quietly closed the door to leave us to talk in private.

CHAPTER 15

The next morning came, and there was excitement in the air. Everyone knew there was a big surprise today, but only Aubrey and Peyton knew what it was. Only thing I told the team was at 1300, we were all going parasailing, and this evening, starting around 2000 hours would be the luau, so everyone was to adjust. "You're eating today to accommodate incredible food and drink. In other words, be hungry."

So 1300 came, and we all met at the marina, where we were boarding two parasailing boats as we had such a large group and we all wanted to go together. Aubrey and the girls and half of the team got into one boat, and me, Rose, and Peyton and the rest of the team got into the second boat.

Step 1 of the surprise began. The first boat was being briefed by Aubrey as soon as we left the docks; my boat would be briefed at the right time. We got cruising out into the beautiful water, soaking up the tropical sunlight and fresh air. The scenery was staggering any which way we looked. Watched dolphins, and we even saw a couple of humpback whales clearing the water as they spouted. Could hear squeals of delight from the other boat as Cindy and Emily stood on the bow with their arms spread wide, as they were splashed from the bows and loving life. Even some of the team were visibly excited and laughing.

Finally, it was time to start launching these guys into the air. Rose was excited and even giddy, but she was also terrified, and it was obvious.

I asked, "Are you ready to go up, love?"

"Oh God, no," she replied. "Let them go first. I want to watch them."

So one at a time, everyone was taking their turns, hooting and hollering as they flew into the air, and even as they reached the five-hundred-feet limit. Both boats were launching at the same time and pretty much running parallel paths. As they were landing back on the boat, Rose was excitedly asking them, "How was it, did you like it?"

Boomer landed and told Rose, "It's like being an eagle, so peaceful. You feel like you are flying on your own almost. You can barely hear the boats or anything but the wind."

Rose looked back at me with a gleam of excitement in her eyes. Then she turned to me and said, "I'm surprised the girls haven't gone up yet. I figured they'd be the first ones up."

I replied, "I don't know. Maybe like you they're afraid and watching everyone else go first."

She laughed nervously and said, "Probably."

It got down to us two, and the crew were changing the saddle from a single to a double so Rose and I could go up together. I was now nervous but not for that flight, as I've parasailed before, but because it was surprise time.

Rose and I sat on the launch deck side by side as the crew was buckling us in. Rose nervously held my hand to the point of cutting off its blood circulation. She was shaking, and those beautiful lips were quivering as I bent into her and tenderly kissed her and smiled. She pulled back, looking into my eyes intensely as I looked deep into her pure soul, and then I yelled to the crew, "Let's get this party started!"

At that, we were launched into the air.

Now I've never wanted to get my ears pierced, but I'm telling you, they got pierced then as Rose was screaming to the top of her lungs in my now-deaf ears.

"Oh my god, oh my god!" she screamed, covering her eyes.

Of course, I was laughing at her response. She, of course, was unaware that the first boat had launched the girls right after we launched and that they were behind us. Step 2 was in play of the surprise.

Finally, Rose stopped screaming and was looking around and loving the serenity of flight. She looked behind us and saw the girls flying behind us having a blast and waving at us. I looked down into both boats and saw Aubrey and Peyton with cameras in their hands recording.

"Oh my god Rip, look at Haleakala, you can't even see the top of it, it's so beautiful, it's majestic!" Rose exclaimed. "The water is crystal clear. It's so beautiful here."

I turned to Rose and replied, "Because you're here, it's the most beautiful place on earth to be right now."

"Aw, babe, thank you. Thank you for all of this."

I looked into her blue eyes and said, "I have to say something, Rose." I looked all somber and serious. "You are my dream; you are my fantasy come to life. The little girl in you makes the little boy in me want to kick over his blocks and come out to play. The love and passion and compassion you have in your heart is unlike anyone I've ever known. Only you could kiss the frozen ground in the winter and make a rose grow. To me, you are larger than life."

Rose had tears welling up in her eyes as I reached behind me.

"So with that said," I told her, "I need to ask you a question."

Her eyes got huge, and her hands went over her mouth as I brought my hand out front with a little black box.

"Rose, will you marry me? I cannot imagine my life, or the girls' lives, without you."

"Yes!" she screamed. "Oh, God, yes, I'll marry you!"

The girls were now flying right close to us, screaming their approval.

"Oh my god, it's so big, Rip," Rose said. She put her hand out for me to put the ring on her finger, but she hit the box accidentally, knocking it out of my hand. She and I both fumbled trying to catch it before losing it, and we watched it fall and hit the water. She was screaming and crying, and the girls were screaming.

I just looked down at the water and shook my head and said, "Damn, I hate it when that happens."

She looked over at me like I was nuts. "Is that all you have to say?" she cried out. "I'm so sorry, Rip, I'm so sorry!"

"It's okay, love, it's okay. Thank God that ring was fake."

"What?" she sputtered. "What do you mean it was fake?" She looked at me in shock as I peered down at the water and reached into my pocket.

I pulled out an identical ring. "This is the real one. It's a two-carat diamond with quarter-carat chips around the setting. Silver ring. That one was just glass. Slowly, give me your hand"

She extended her shaking hand out, and I gently but firmly slipped the ring onto her finger. I watched her eyes and saw her beautiful smile light up the already sunny sky, and I fell in love with my soul mate all over again.

"So, this was the surprise you've been planning?" she asked.

As we were slowly being reeled back in, we could hear whistles and claps coming from the boats.

"It's part of it," I replied.

"They all knew about this?" she asked.

"No, only Peyton and Aubrey knew. Everyone else found out just before you did." I laughed.

We landed on the deck as the first boat came long side us, and we tied off with them.

"This is the other half of the surprise."

Rose looked around, and one of the boat crewmen came from behind the others in the other boat with a Bible in his hand.

Rose was speechless, looking over everyone's faces smiling back at her and looking back at me. "Now? We are getting married right now?"

"If you want to, Rose," I said. "We have the preacher, we have the bridesmaids and the best men in the world right here as our witnesses and family, and I have my best man right here."

Boomer came walking up and hugged Rose tight.

"This is crazy," Rose said. "But so far, this whole venture with you has been crazy, so yes. Let's do this!" She looked at the girls and said, "I can never replace your mom, but are you okay with me being your stepmom?"

They both looked at Rose with excitement and replied yes and hugged her tight.

"Then I want you both to be my maids of honor."

The preacher spoke up, asking, "Do we have the rings?"

Boomer said yes as he showed his, and Aubrey handed the girls Rose's wedding band. Both girls held the ring.

The wedding went off without a hitch, and we made our bond permanent on those boats in the middle of the bay of Maui, with Haleakala looming as a backdrop in beautiful Hawaii.

* * *

Upon arrival to the luau, we had the beach and the tiki bar blocked off to outsiders as a private event. The guys managed to get a couple of dozen local ladies to come join the party, and they were already in full-swing party mode. It was great to see them having a good time and blowing off steam.

The luau company was doing a superb job. Pig was roasting over an open pit, tiki torches were burning, and there was one hell of a buffet of incredible food. Fire eaters and dancers entertained us and showing us a great time. The native girls in grass skirts were doing their ancestors' dance and teaching Aubrey, Peyton, Emily, Cindy, and Rose how to hula. Even a couple of the guys donned grass skirts and were trying to follow along. After a couple of piña coladas, I was up there joining in and having a ball. This luau/reception was the best ever, and even the workers were having the time of their lives.

As it was winding down a little, Rose and I snuck off and took a walk along the beach hand in hand in the moonlight. The stars were bright glistening off the ocean as a warm gentle breeze blew across the sand. We stopped and gazed out into the ocean, and I stood behind Rose with my arms wrapped around her waist and held her.

"How are you feeling, Mrs. Johnson?" I asked.

"I feel absolutely amazing, Mr. Johnson, thank you for asking," she replied. "I don't want this to ever end."

I buried my face more into her neck and softly whispered, "It's only just begun, lover." I tenderly kissed her soft neck as she sighed.

"Careful there, buster," she said. "You may get something started you can't finish right now."

I gently nudged her and said, "Look over there. There's a lifeguard tower over there." I chuckled.

She joyfully laughed and replied, "What are we, sixteen again?"

"Well, not quite, but—"

"No," she snorted, laughing.

"No?" I replied, laughing.

"No," she said more firmly. She turned and faced me and kissed my cheek. "Maybe tomorrow night," she flirtatiously replied. She walked off back toward the luau.

The next morning, we gathered up everything for a day at the beach, and the girls were excited, especially Cindy because Bull was going to start teaching her to surf. We arrived at the beach to find most of the guys and some of the ladies they had picked up the day before already set up. Some were playing Frisbee, others swimming and bodysurfing, and some with the girls on their shoulders trying to knock each other over.

I was watching the activities when Rose softly said, "Rip, look."

I turned to see where Rose was looking. Off toward the cluster of palms came Bull wearing nothing but Speedos.

"Holy sh——t!" I exclaimed.

Bull looked like Mr. Universe. The man was ripped from head to toe; even his *ripples* were ripped. He came walking toward us carrying two surfboards, his and a pink smaller one. Cindy saw him coming and ran off, yelling, "Mr. Bull!"

Bull stopped and knelt down to her, still towering over her. She excitedly hugged his neck as he explained, "This is for you, kitten. This is your board, so you have to take good care of it. I'll show you how and how to wax it."

Cindy's little face was full of excitement as she turned toward us, showing us her board. "Look what my Mr. Bull got me, my very own surfboard!"

We were watching Bull as he had her standing on the board in the sand, showing her the proper stance and balancing techniques. Bull then told Cindy, "You wait right here, I'm going to go catch a wave and show you. You pay attention to what I'm doing, okay?"

"Okay, Mr. Bull," she replied.

Bull grabbed his board and took off running into the surf. He jumped ace down onto the board, paddling out with a couple of other surfers. He got out to where the swales began and sat up so he could see the swales as they came in. He spotted what looked to be a good one and began paddling with the wave just as we heard some screaming from out in the water.

I searched the water as there were many swimmers, and finally, I could see several people panicking, heading toward shore, screaming and yelling "Shark!"

The whistles began as the lifeguards sprang into action, running toward their wave runners. It appeared all our people were safe, except Bull. We could see thrashing in the water where the shark was at, attacking a swimmer. The lifeguards were just entering the water, and they had a distance to cover to get to the man.

Bull saw what was going on, and he turned his board, heading straight for the shark. He was crouched down and picking up speed as fast as he could go, and just as he approached it, he took the board to the top of the wave and leaped high into the air with full momentum. Looking like a superhero, he raised his fist and came down with all his might, driving his massive fist into the shark.

Well, after the initial impact, we couldn't see the action, but we could see heads and then a tail and fins. There was one hell of a fight going on. Meantime, the wave runners arrived and were pulling the swimmer out of the water as the fight continued. Two of the wave runners were heading toward shore as a couple of ambulances arrived on the beach. The swimmer had lost an arm and was bleeding out as the paramedics got to working on him immediately.

I looked out into the water. It appeared the fight was over, but I wasn't sure who won. The third lifeguard was still out there idling in circles, and then we could see Bull coming toward shore slowly.

Sh——t, I thought. *He must be injured, but why isn't the life-guard helping him come ashore?*

Well, we soon got the answer when Bull got his feet on the ground: Bull had towed the shark with him and was dragging it onto the beach.

The onlookers were gasping to see this bloodied monster as Bull was half-carrying it and dropped it into the sand.

"I need a knife!" Bull yelled.

Cowboy grabbed a knife from his bag and ran to Bull and handed it to him.

Rose asked, "What's he going to do, Rip? It's already dead."

I reached down and turned Cindy's head away and looked at Rose. "He's going to try to recover that man's arm."

Rose replied, "He's going to *what*? Oh, god, no. Come on, Cindy, let's go for a walk." She grabbed up Emily, Peyton, and Aubrey and walked off toward the restrooms.

In a single thrust, Bull gutted the shark and reached inside, feeling for the arm. I grabbed our cooler and dumped all the contents into the sand except for the ice and took it to Bull, as he found and pulled out the arm still intact but slightly shredded. We put it in the cooler and gave it to the paramedics; hopefully, they'd be able to save it.

Bull was a mess, and the stench from the shark was strong, and many onlookers were grossed out as Bull walked by them covered in blood and guts. The second paramedic unit started tending to Bull and checking out his injuries, which turned out to be very minor. More than what we could say about the fourteen-foot shark that he had just killed with his bare hands.

A surfer approached Bull, carrying Bull's board.

"Dude," he said. "That was gnarly, man. Like, you tore that monster up. My ol' lady recorded the whole thing, man. You're a f——cking hero. Damn!"

Paramedics released Bull, shaking their heads, saying they have never seen anything like it.

Bull looked up at me and said, "I'm going to go shower, boss."

We bumped fists as he stood up and turned and walked away. It was only then that I realized Bull was butt-ass naked. That shark had eaten his Speedos.

Throwing Cowboy a towel, I yelled and laughed, "Nice ass, Bull!"

He responded by shaking it at me, and he got quite the applause from the beach crowd. Cowboy caught up with Bull, handing him the towel and about crying; he was laughing so hard. Bull just threw the towel over his shoulder and kept on strutting to the showers.

* * *

Through the week, we ventured all around the islands sight-seeing, including stopping at the *USS Arizona* memorial at Pearl Harbor. It was a very somber experience for us all as we witnessed a funeral service of a Pearl Harbor survivor being taken out, and his ashes were committed to the memorial with his brothers who died on December 7, 1941.

Cindy's surfing lessons were going well, and she was having the time of her life. Emily was spending a lot of time with Aubrey and Peyton as they took her under their wing. Aubrey had been abducted herself before and gone through the experiences as Emily, and was able to relate and console her.

The days went fast as most vacations do, and it was almost time to return to reality.

Rose and I were in our room after a long hot day, getting ready for bed, when the phone rang. It was Special Agent Blye.

I answered the phone. "Yes, sir."

"Sounds like you guys are having a great time out there. How's Bull doing? I see the news of his little fight with a shark. Was he injured, or did he just eat the shark?" he asked.

Laughing, I replied, "No, he's fine, just minor scrapes and cuts. What can I do for you?"

"Have you been watching the news?" he asked.

"No, I haven't," I replied. "Why?"

"The situation in Denver has escalated, and the governor won't allow the National Guard to come in and assist the police, and to make it worse, the mayor won't even allow the police to use force. The police union is about to push for a blue flu epidemic. These thugs have established an autonomous zone and barricaded themselves in, and they've executed nine police officers so far. There are riots every night, and most of downtown Denver looks like a war zone."

"What do you want us to do about it?" I asked.

"Can you breach their zone and do your thing to, let's say, *dishearten* them? The police chief said he's willing to ignore the mayor's orders if the right buttons are pushed."

"Let me talk to my men. We'll be leaving tomorrow night to head back. I have a couple of ideas."

The next morning, we headed to the beach for the last time and were greeted by two of the lifeguards from the shark attack.

"Aloha," they said.

"We wanted to thank you again for saving Kyle's life," one said.

They turned and addressed Bull directly. They reached out and shook his hand.

"How's he doing?" I asked.

"He's stable. They reattached his arm, but it's too soon to tell if it'll work. So far, so good. He would really like to thank you personally before you leave. It would mean a lot to him and boost his morale."

"I'm sure we can get over there to see him before we leave tonight," I replied.

"Great. Well, you people enjoy your day. We've got to get to work. Aloha."

I turned to Cindy and said, "Well, baby, you ready to go show us what you got out there?"

Cindy excitedly nodded her head yes and turned to Bull, who knelt before her.

"Just remember what I taught you, balance is the key," Bull said. "Go get it, kitten."

Cindy grabbed her board and ran off toward the surf. I looked up at Bull as he stood and turned toward me.

"No worries, Rip. I'm going with her. No sharks will touch my kitten." He grabbed his board and followed Cindy.

They dove onto their boards and paddled out to wait for their wave. Didn't take long, and they laid down and started paddling as a swale began raising behind them.

Rose came up behind me and wrapped her arms around me. Emily came long side us and leaned into us as we put our arms around her.

"I love you, guys," Emily choked out, her emotions overwhelming her.

"We love you way more," I replied, as I squeezed her tight.

"I know, Daddy," she replied.

Cindy now leaped to her feet. A little unsteady at first, but she quickly recovered, and Bull leaped to his feet as well, surfing right alongside her, coaching her along the way.

"Look at her go," Emily squealed.

"Oh my god, Rip, look at our little girl go," Rose said excitedly, as she squeezed her hug.

"Yes, my baby is growing up," I replied, as I watched her go, with her monstrous Mr. Bull by her side.

ABOUT THE AUTHOR

Started in law enforcement at the young age of fifteen. Served in the military for eight years in weapons and security. Been to multiple countries. Determined that our country may not be perfect but by far the best. Served on a sheriff's department for ten years. Got into private security and bodyguard work with multiple celebrities.

I wrote short stories as a child, and close friends enticed me to write a book. Some of these events are true, and some are not and are purely for entertainment purposes.

I hope you enjoy this book and the following books of this series.

Printed in the USA
CPSIA information can be obtained
at www.ICGtesting.com
LVHW090609130524
779900LV00002B/335

9 781662 485121